THE SCA

BOOK FIVE OF

CW00841321

Robert Ryan

Cover design by www.damonza.com

ISBN: 9798594317239
(print edition)

Trotting Fox Press

Contents

1. The Shadow Blade

It had been a morning of terror. Druilgar took satisfaction in that, yet still he was troubled by other matters. The weight of kingship rested heavily on him.

Things would grow worse before they became better though. If Faladir were to be made anew, it must be broken first. So too the rest of the world. A sword could not be made unless the iron from which it was wrought endured both furnace and hammer. And he would be the smith to forge his people into a conquering nation, for the world beckoned and wide realms were ripe for the plucking.

Could his people not see this? It was true that some did, but others resisted. The rebels had struck at him several times, and still it burned his soul that Caludreth had been rescued. Or was it even worse that they had now toppled the statue of their king, his own likeness?

Perhaps that was worse. But it was also vanity, and he knew it. Graver by far had been the rough words cut into the stone of the plinth on which the statue had rested. *The seventh knight comes.*

That was more dangerous than any insult. It was a promise, and it brought hope to the people that the prophesy of old would come to pass.

The people had seen it too. By their hundreds they had flooded into the square where the statue had stood, preparing for the markets. Soldiers had chiseled away those hateful words, and now, by noon, the plinth itself had been removed. Yet the damage was done and mouths passed on what eyes had seen.

But he had given them something else to think about. There was satisfaction in that. He had released some of his swelling army upon the populace. Elù-draks, were-beasts and other creatures of legend had haunted the city and preyed on the vulnerable. This was the first time they had done so in daylight hours, and even here in the Tower of the Stone he had heard screams and felt the waves of fear that he had unleashed.

But as ordered, when noon came the assault had ceased. Fear was a weapon to be used sparingly. Too much, and he risked civil war. Not enough, and the rebels would be emboldened. He thought one morning of terror had got that balance right.

What should come next? It was a question that vexed him. His thoughts were interrupted though. He sat, cross-legged, in the uppermost chamber of the tower where the Morleth Stone rested. A knock on the great door sounded dully throughout the chamber.

He knew who it was, for he had summoned him not long since.

"Enter."

The door swung open. There was a ritual for this, but Druilgar ignored it. The rite was intended as a guard to the stone, but that was no longer necessary. Not while he was here, for his powers had grown and no one would dare attempt theft. It would be certain death, for none could stand against him now, either with blade or magic.

Barlan came into the room, closing the door behind him. He was a huge man, well above six feet and heavy set with it, including a large belly. Not for the first time Druilgar marveled that such a big man could move with grace and speed. But he could. He also wondered how this man had ever become a knight, for he had a personality to match his build. He was loud and boisterous, and his laughter often boomed. He would slap men on the back, either noble or commoner, and laugh freely at some jest. But few saw the cold edge to his gaze that no laughter ever lit. Nor did most people know that this was his preferred way of killing. Distract with a friendly joke and then stab unexpectedly with a concealed dagger.

Druilgar liked him. He was hard not to like. But he never turned his back on him.

"Greetings, First Knight Druilgar," the man said in his deep voice. If he had been surprised that the ritual of identification at the opening of the door had been forgone, he gave no indication of it.

"Hail, Knight Barlan."

The king gestured with his hand for the other man to sit. There were no chairs here, except under the old desk over to the side that knights had once used to write poetry. A waste of a warrior's time, if ever there was one. It had been another of Aranloth's strange ideas, and Druilgar wondered that the wise could be so stupid.

Barlan sat gracefully on the bearskin rug, and he bowed his head in respect. Before them both was the iron box, rusted and ancient, in which the Morleth Stone rested. The lid was open, as it always was these days. And a sheen of light came from the stone, but it was mostly quiet at the moment.

It was not always so. Sometimes strange lights burned and flashed within it, and Druilgar wondered what was inside. Sometimes he fancied it was its own world within the stone, and warriors and sorcerers fought within it. A foolish thought, but something *did* cause those lights and he had no better explanation.

Barlan raised his head after a little while. His long red hair fell back, rough and uncombed. His red beard could do with a trim also, but Druilgar did not rebuke him as once he would have. Better that he looked a simple warrior than a Morleth Knight. Subterfuge had its uses, and he would not long remain in the city where people knew him. Druilgar had picked him to fulfil another purpose.

"You summoned me, First Knight?" the man said. No doubt he wondered why, and typical to his ways he had gotten straight to the point.

"Indeed. Events move apace, and I have need of you."

The knight made no answer to that, and Druilgar liked it. Barlan was one to wait and see what was asked of him before he ventured to comment. Others would ask questions that only interfered with what facts needed to be brought out first.

"You know we seek the girl Ferla," Druilgar continued. It was a statement rather than a question. All the knights knew, more or less, what missions were underway and their importance.

"I know," Barlan replied.

"This much is news though," Druilgar said. "Savanest had her. He captured her for a while when she spirit walked, and he bound her with magic intended to fill her with fear when they met in the flesh. He was close on her trail, and they would have met by now."

Barlan whistled through his teeth. "She knew how to spirit walk? That's surprising."

"It is. But more surprisingly still, I have not had further word from Savanest."

Barlan pursed his lips and raised a bushy eyebrow at that, as well he might.

"He is dead, then? Otherwise he would have reported her capture."

Druilgar did not like to admit that another knight had failed because it reflected badly on himself. But it was so.

"He is dead, or something…"

"What does that mean?"

Druilgar shook his head. "I don't know. When I reach out to commune with him, the magic is scattered and confused. It does not feel like it did with Lindercroft. With him, I knew he was dead. But Savanest? Well, it doesn't matter. One way or another he is lost to us."

Barlan contemplated that in silence for a few moments. For all his friendly manner, there was no love lost between him and the other knights. Their demise only brought opportunity to him. Yet it was still sobering to learn that a skilled comrade had been defeated.

"How is it," he asked at length, "that the enemy is capable of this? First Lindercroft and now Savanest. It should not be possible."

It was a good question, and one that Druilgar had struggled with himself.

"It's the prophecy at work. Or destiny, or fate, or whatever name you wish to give it. The world is driven in a certain direction, and forces are at play that cannot be denied."

Barlan ran a hand through his straggly beard and screwed up his face in thought.

"But if the seventh knight is destined to come against us, then how can we win?"

Druilgar looked at him sideways, and a wave of displeasure welled up. How could a knight even contemplate defeat?

"The seventh knight is destined, and we can do nothing about that. But nowhere in the prophecy does it say the knight will prevail. Only that he, or as we have since learned, she, will come against us. Our fault has been to try to kill her. Instead, as Savanest was beginning to do, we must look instead toward making her one of us. After all, who better to fill the place of one of the knights she has defeated than herself?"

What he did not say was that it had been his own fault that they had tried to kill her. Instead of going to Dromdruin Village with swords and fire, they should have gone as friends to win trust. But that was an error that could not be rectified now. Yet even there, the prophecy was at work. Had they not done as they did, the woman Ferla would not have commenced the training needed to become a knight. So it was not his fault at all, really. It was destined.

Barlan took up his line of thought. "How can we make her one of us? Surely it is too late for that."

"Nothing is beyond us now," Druilgar said, and he glanced at the Morleth Stone. "Osahka guides us, and its power is greater by far than we have ever guessed. If we bring her before it, it will turn her to our cause."

"Can we do so, though?" Barlan asked. "If she guesses our purpose, she sounds to me like one who would rather die than be captured."

"She is indeed. And I believe she knows our purpose. That will make it harder, for she will die in battle rather than endure our plans for her. But I have a means to deal with that."

Barlan was suddenly curious. "What means is that?"

"First," Druilgar answered, "I shall give you your mission. For this is become your quest. But you need to know what is happening so you can take the necessary steps."

Barlan gave a slight nod. He did not like the answer to his question being forestalled, but he had also instantly grasped that he was about to receive an opportunity to rise above his brother knights.

Druilgar went on. "Now that Savanest is lost, the girl is lost to us too. We'll need to find her again before we can implement the next necessary step."

"That will be my task, then?"

"Yes. In this, you may need to work with Sofanil. Much depends on what happens with him and how quickly he completes his own task."

"He is looking for the one called Faran?"

Druilgar grinned. "No longer. He has found him, and the noose there is close to slipping tight."

This was bad news for Barlan, for the quicker Sofanil fulfilled his own task the more readily he would move on to finding Ferla. That might mean sharing credit for capturing her, and that was the last thing the big man would want. Yet still, not even a flicker of such thoughts crossed his face. That was well, for while Druilgar wanted the knights to vie against each other for supremacy, they had to be able to hide their feelings in order to cooperate when that was required.

"There's another thing you should know," Druilgar said. "Savanest was Sofanil's brother. Not only his knight-brother, but also by blood. This you probably knew. It was no great secret, though they seldom spoke of it."

"I knew," Barlan answered.

"Good. His brother's demise will give Sofanil extra motive to move against Ferla. If he captures her, she will regret what she has done. But I think you can handle Ferla, and I still want Faran killed. There is something about him that troubles me, even if he is not the seventh knight. So I don't want Sofanil distracted. Not yet."

Barlan understood. He looked a big warrior, all muscles and no brains, but his mind was sharp.

"If I speak with him, you do not wish me to reveal what you have said about Savanest?"

"Exactly so. Say nothing. I will tell him in due course, when he needs to know and not before."

Barlan nodded briskly. "Then I shall make ready and commence my search for the girl. She won't elude me. But if she forces a fight, then it is possible she will be killed."

"That must *not* happen," Druilgar commanded. As he spoke, he drew something from beneath his cloak. He knew what it was, but Barlan did not. Yet the knight must have sensed the magic of the thing, for his eyes fixed on it intently.

Druilgar looked at it himself. It was a dagger in a sheath. The hilt of the weapon was of ebony hardwood, heavy to the touch and polished to a gleam. The blade was covered in an ancient scabbard marked by eldritch runes stitched in gold thread. They were much like the runes of the elves, but not quite.

He did not unsheathe the blade. Instead, he placed the knife on the floor between them.

"Pick it up," he commanded. "Unsheathe the weapon, but if you value your life do not touch the edge. The sheath is there for a reason, and so too the magic sealed in the runes."

Barlan hesitated. He certainly sensed the magic in the thing, and that was small wonder. It was a talisman of great potency.

The knight reached out and took the hilt in his pale-skinned hand. He held the weapon before him, feeling its weight and probing it with his mind. That, Druilgar knew, would avail him nothing. It was a weapon and a sorcery beyond his experience.

"It's called a shadow blade," Druilgar told him. "Remove it from the sheath, but I warn you again, on no account touch the edges."

Barlan moved with great caution. He removed the sheath slowly and revealed the blade. It was a thing of wicked beauty, and its double-edged length came to a gracefully sloping point. The metal was slender and delicate. This was no rough and tumble blade intended for battle. It was a work of art. Or had been.

But magic infused it as well. The steel was blacker even than the ebony handle, and thin lines of green light twined and moved below its shiny surface. And more runes were upon it, different from those on the sheath. These were of silver and it seemed the green lights flowed around them but never touched them.

"It's a thing of beauty," Barlan whispered.

"So it is. Cover it now, so that we can talk in safety."

The knight sheathed the blade. He did it carefully too, though he did not know why. But he still obeyed his king's instructions, even if he did not understand them. That was just as well.

"So, what does this shadow blade do?" Barlan asked. "Obviously, it's an artifact from the ancient world. No one has the skill to make such a thing now, and I can sense the great magic within it. But how did you acquire it and what is its purpose?"

Druilgar glanced at the Morleth Stone. It had been Osahka who had led him to the blade. But there was no need to recount how he had left the city and dug up an ancient grave to obtain it. No, that had not been a pleasant experience. But the knight needed to know none of that.

"We discussed before that the woman Ferla would rather die than become one of us. But become one of us she will. The blade will ensure it." He glanced again at the Morleth Stone, and he had the feeling it was listening to him speak. It was disconcerting. Or was it reassuring? More and more he believed it was the latter. The stone was always on his mind lately, and that was like basking in the warmth of a fire when the cold winter wind howled outside.

"The blade," he said, "needs only to cut the skin and draw blood. That is all. It is not for killing. Indeed, it cannot kill at all."

11

Barlan frowned. "It seems to me that the blade is long enough to reach the heart. So too the edges sharp enough to sever an artery. Surely it can kill, though the magic in it exists for another purpose."

Druilgar laughed grimly. "This is one such blade that even if its tip reaches the heart, it cannot kill. The magic in it makes it so. What it does is to draw the person cut by it partly into the void. In a sense, they are dead. But in a sense, they are also still alive. The blade traps them between worlds. They will endure a shadow existence. But that is all that is required for Ferla. Osahka will be even more easily able to turn her and to make her one of us. And the last refuge available to her, death, will not be an option."

Barlan stiffened. He would have known the weapon he had been given was dangerous, but now he appreciated that it was even worse than anything he could have contemplated. It was a weapon that should he be careless with could deliver him to the same fate planned for their enemy. He held it as though it were a poisonous viper in his hand, but then overcoming his fear he undid his belt and slid the leather through the loop attached to the sheath.

"I'll not fail," the knight said.

"Best that you do not," Druilgar answered, and he looked back at the Morleth Stone. The audience was over.

Barlan did not hesitate. He stood, and walked from the chamber leaving Druilgar alone. That was just as well, for he had much to think about.

His chief problem was the rebels in the city. Once the seventh knight was subverted, all hope of overthrowing him was ended, for the prophecy would be dead. Yet that would take some time. What could he do about the rebels in the meanwhile?

He had to do something. They must be found and attacked. He would not find all of them, but their impudence could not go unpunished. He would not allow their crimes to stand against him, nor would it be good policy. He must send a message to them and all who supported them. This morning's terror was a good start, but it must not end there.

2. A Trap is Set

Of the death-sleep of the lòhrens, Kareste had told Faran little.

That did not mean he had not tried to coax information out of her. But even though his skill with magic had blossomed, it seemed there were always levels of knowledge, and he was not yet ready to break through to that echelon.

He tried once more as they passed through a group of scrubby trees, their leaves blown away by winter winds and their bare branches reaching starkly for the crisp blue sky.

"How can Aranloth sleep in the tombs, if he isn't able to say the charm that keeps the harakgar at bay?"

Kareste did not change expression, and it seemed that she would give him no more answer on this subject than she normally did, but she surprised him with her reply this time.

"The death-sleep is well named," she said, stepping over the trunk of a tree blown down by a recent gale. "Aranloth's spirit drifts between worlds, partly here and partly in the void. He is so close to death that the harakgar deem him so, and they let him be."

"How then does it enable him to heal and—"

But she strode ahead up a short bank and ignored him. He scrambled up after her, using the low-hanging branch of a tree to help pull himself up, but when he drew level with her she had turned around.

He did not interrupt her. Instead, he joined her in looking out over their backtrail from this slightly higher vantage.

They saw nothing. Nothing out of place, anyway. It was a wild land behind them, mostly grassy slopes but here and there little clumps of trees. Faran wondered where Ferla was just now, and if the part of Alithoras she trod was like this. Probably it was, for they could not be that far apart yet.

They had traveled for five days, warily, looking for signs of pursuit just as they did now. They had seen nothing though.

It was a relief, yet he could not help but worry for Ferla. If he was not being pursued, did it mean the enemy had found her?

There was no way to know, and no way to ease his disquiet. He would not be happy until he saw her again, but that would be a long while in the future.

Abruptly, Kareste turned and commenced the march once more. She used her staff to help her walk, but she did not need to. She had not even used it to help her up the bank. But she was tired. Of that, Faran was sure. He was himself, for they had set a fast pace.

They had traveled swiftly since parting with the others, and that was days ago. They were well past the halfway point to the tombs, and they had bypassed the valley of the lake, skirting wide around it. They had no wish to go there. Faran in particular had no desire to see the ruins of the cottage where he had been so happy with Ferla. Better that he kept his memories of the place as it was.

There were only two days to go until they reached their destination, and he was dreading that. The harakgar scared him, and he did not mind admitting that to himself.

They kept going through the afternoon, and just as dusk fell about them with a cold wind blowing, they found

15

a dry riverbed, all sand and silt, whose steep slopes offered shelter from the weather.

It was the first night that they lit a fire. The cold demanded it, and that there had been no sign of pursuit made it possible. Faran built it, and he used the driest of timber that would not smoke much, and what there was would be dispersed by the branches of the tree under which he lit it.

Even with all these precautions, they used the heat only briefly to warm up and to cook a sparse meal. When they were done, Faran kicked sand over it and put out the flames.

When he sat down again, Kareste spoke. "Fear not, Faran. Better days are ahead. One day we'll be safe again, and the king will be defeated and you'll be reunited with Ferla. All this will seem but a dream."

He was not so sure of that. "You believe Ferla will fulfill the prophecy then?"

Kareste shrugged. "Prophecies are just words. Nothing is fixed in stone. But I know Ferla, and I know you. I believe you'll succeed, and you don't need fate to guide you. You are who you are, and that is all that's required."

"Wasn't it Aranloth who gave the prophecy long ago? I wonder if he would agree with you."

At that, Kareste laughed. "Aranloth believes less in prophecy than anyone."

"How can that be? He was the one who spoke it?"

Kareste rolled her staff to and fro in her lap. It was a gesture she often displayed, and Faran had learned it meant she was thinking deeply about something.

"He has heard, and uttered, more prophecies than anyone," she continued. "So he knows they never turn out quite as expected. A prophecy is no more than a vision spoken aloud, and all lòhrens have visions of the future. But the thing is, there are many possible futures. And something changed before it happens, even the smallest of things, can alter the direction of the future just as moving forward or backward causes your shadow to shrink or lengthen."

Faran was not sure what to think of that. He might have preferred it more when he thought that Ferla was destined to be the seventh knight. But at the same time, he knew also that the seventh knight would only fight the evil of the Morleth Stone. There had never been a guarantee of victory at the end.

A gust of wind blew through their dry camp, rattling dead leaves and shifting the sand in eddies and swirls. Faran paid no heed to it, but Kareste looked up and tilted her head as though listening. Then she stood, leaning on her staff and looked into the starlit dark.

Slowly, Faran stood himself, and he drew his sword. Despite Kareste's casual posture, he sensed that she was poised for battle.

Nothing happened, but his sense of unease increased. Then the wind gusted again, and the rattle of dry leaves was loud. Sand swirled through the air, rising up, and it formed a shape.

In moments, a knight stood before them. Faran did not know which one he was, but he knew a Morleth Knight when he saw one. It did not matter that the image was made of sand held together into shape by magic. There was an arrogance to the stance, and a confidence born of countless victories. Even in the dark, and made of only sand and sorcery, it still looked almost like a real person.

"You are Knight Sofanil," Kareste said quietly. "But you are not welcome here."

The knight gave a slight bow. "I'm honored that you know my name. Perhaps my fame has reached you?"

Kareste smiled. "Fame? Rather I would say infamy, for you have forgone your sacred trust and serve the evil your forbears fought to defeat."

"And yet you still know my name. So fame, infamy, or something in between, you have made a point of acquainting yourself with my reputation."

Kareste straightened a little, but she still leaned on the staff.

"I know your reputation, and your history. Aranloth said you were the subtlest of the knights, and the most intelligent. He warned me against you, and considered you the most dangerous of all our enemies. Except, of course, the king. His power is grown far greater than your own."

Faran did not speak. Kareste was stronger in magic than he was, and wiser by far. But he saw her tactic here. She had complimented the man, and then had humbled him. For Aranloth had made it clear that all the knights had become prideful, and they vied against each other. Not only that, they would also supplant the king in a moment if they could. But the power of the Morleth Stone was his, and envy of that gnawed at them, for they would make it theirs if they could. The lure of it was strong, and it burned them that another had what they did not.

Sofanil laughed, and it was a sound carefree as any that Faran had ever heard.

"You seek to divide me from my king. Yet I am but a humble servant, free of ambition. I serve the king, truly and faithfully, and he will be pleased with me."

There was a threat in that, and Faran knew it. What had he done that the king would be pleased with? Surely it must involve some plan set in motion against those he pursued. Kareste also must have sensed it, for she straightened fully and took her weight off the staff as though she might use it.

18

Sofanil spoke before she acted though. "I am but an image, lady, and I know you have the power to dispel me. Please, do not trouble yourself. I shall leave you shortly."

It was the first time that Faran had ever seen Kareste at a loss for words. The knight was polite, even friendly, and that was not something that they anticipated. But it was in its way even more chilling.

"What then is your purpose here, Sofanil?"

The knight smiled. "Merely to meet my adversaries, and that I have done. Sleep well, for a new day is coming, and it will dawn over all Alithoras."

Even as he spoke, the wind gusted again and the sand that made up the form of Sofanil fell back to the ground.

Faran was even more uneasy now that the knight was gone. Again, there had been a threat in those final words. It was something personal, referring to him and Kareste. A change that he saw in their lives, but behind it was also a greater threat to the whole land. The king, or rather the Morleth Stone, would never be satisfied with Faladir.

Kareste did not move. She stared silently at the sand that had fallen to the shadowy ground. Nothing made any sound, nor did the wind gust again.

"He is gone, isn't he?" Faran asked.

Kareste stirred at last. "Of course. He is gone. But he still troubles me. What did he want here?"

"He said he wanted to meet us."

She frowned at that. "So he said, but whatever his manner, he means us nothing but harm and every word he says must be considered a lie."

"Do you think he knows where we are?"

"Perhaps. He has to be close to appear to us as he did, but that doesn't mean he knows exactly where we are. But why appear at all? He could simply have tried to close in on us in the flesh without giving us forewarning."

Faran could not guess Sofanil's motives. But he knew how he felt himself.

"I don't like it."

Kareste glanced at him, and he saw, despite her usual unbreakable calm, worry on her face.

"I don't like it, either."

They set off after that. There would be no night's rest for them, even if they sorely needed it. Better to be far away from this spot by dawn.

Despite their tiredness, they moved swiftly. The night grew old around them, and they did not rest save for brief spells every hour or so. Then, they looked behind them into the impenetrable dark, but they saw nothing.

Clouds rose up out of the east and threatened rain. They blocked the faint light of stars and it grew truly dark, but no rain fell. Yet the night was cold, and the travelers moved ahead into the shadows with their cloaks tightly about them and their hoods pulled up.

As shadows they were themselves. They crossed the landscape like wild animals, wary and cautious, shy of being seen and skilled enough that they likely would not be.

Faran stumbled ahead, but Kareste strode swiftly and showed no sign of the exhaustion that she must feel. He was reminded of Aranloth then, for like him she could draw on reserves of willpower that were greater than that of a normal person. Or, perhaps, she had some method of sustaining herself with magic. Likely both, yet she saw his tiredness and called a halt in the dark hours before dawn.

With gratitude, Faran threw himself down on the soft grass and slept. It would not be long, that he knew. But it would be something and whatever it was would be enough. He was young and strong, and he could get by on little sleep.

But Kareste did not lie down. She walked a few paces back the way they had come, and there she stood, leaning on her staff and gazing out into the dark. She kept watch, and surely one of them had to. But he was amazed at her strength, and he knew if not for her, and for Aranloth in the past, the enemy would long since have killed him.

3. Evil Stirs

Dawn broke over the land, and the light of it woke Faran from his short sleep.

Kareste stood in just the same place that she had when he had fallen asleep. Like a statue she was, resolute and enduring.

"Did you get any rest?" he asked.

She stirred and turned toward him. "I'm a lòhren, Faran. I have learned to rest even when I'm awake."

He did not doubt that was true. Yet still it could be no match for proper sleep.

"Why don't you sleep a little while now. I can keep watch."

She smiled at him. "Thank you, but it isn't needed. Nor do we have the time. Sofanil is a crafty foe, and we can afford no delays."

Faran stood and looked out over their backtrail. There seemed nothing amiss. But that did not make him feel better.

They ate a quick breakfast then, and their supplies were getting low so they made it a sparse one too. Soon, he would put his skill as a hunter to use. But with Sofanil on their trail, he dare not risk it yet. Once they had come out of the tombs though, and lost the enemy, it would be a matter of urgency to find food.

He grew despondent at the thought of the tombs. Certainly, they were a place that Sofanil could not follow them. They would be safe from him inside, and how easy it was to think that they could lose him there and emerge elsewhere at some point he could not find them. But the tombs merely replaced one enemy with another and one set of problems with a different group altogether.

The harakgar were more dangerous by far than a Morleth Knight, and even with the charm to protect themselves he knew they were always only one mistake away from death. But he put those thoughts aside. It was part of his training to acknowledge risk, and then not to dwell on it. If he allowed himself to do that, his problems would only grow bigger in his mind. He forced himself to think of something else.

He was glad when they broke camp though. Once they were on the move and concentrating on day-to-day issues such as the best trail to follow that was easiest to traverse but also offered the greatest concealment, his greater problems receded into the background and the lesser ones distracted his mind from them.

They did not set the fast pace of last night. Rather, in the daylight, they moved more cautiously. But they still traveled quickly, and despite the coolness of the morning he began to sweat freely.

Kareste, usually in the lead, fell back to walk beside him.

"Something isn't quite right, Faran."

The comment resonated with him. "I know. What Sofanil said disturbs me. Or better still, what he didn't say disturbs me. There were no overt threats. There was no real purpose to his visitation."

Kareste ran a hand through her hair, and it was more a sign of frustration than anything else.

"Exactly. What he said and did seemed to have no real purpose. There was a smugness to him as well. But this much I know. Aranloth described him as the smartest of all the knights. Just because we haven't discovered his purpose doesn't mean he didn't have one. I'm sure he did."

23

The land through which they walked was one of gentle slopes and pockets of trees. It was a fair country, but Faran eyed it with suspicion. He sensed danger, and it was clear that Kareste did as well.

"Perhaps," he said, "we're looking at this the wrong way. Sofanil seemed to make no threat, and seemed to prompt no action from us. But let's turn that around. What if he wanted us to do what we were already doing?"

Kareste slowed her pace. "What we were doing was heading toward the tombs. But he cannot know that."

"Can't he? What if he does? What if he merely guesses where we're heading by the direction that we travel?"

This time Kareste stopped walking completely, and she turned to face him.

"You raise a good point. And our action, that he prompted, even if we did not realize it, was to keep going as we were. Worse, our attention has been behind us all this while because we feared pursuit."

Faran felt the cold clutch of fear on his heart. "It begins to make sense now. He ensured we kept going in the exact direction that we already were, and distracted us from what lies ahead. Do you think he's set an ambush for us?"

Kareste did not answer straight away. Instead, she looked out into the country that lay before them. There was nothing out of place. There was no cause for concern. Yet still the quiet land now seemed to be brooding rather than look peaceful. It held hidden menace rather than tranquility.

"The more I think this through, the more I think we've walked right into his trap. Or nearly. If we had, it would have sprung tight about us already. But if there is one, it must be close."

"What then can we do? Retreat? But if we're wrong, we'll end up rushing back toward him."

She looked at him and grinned. "Sofanil thinks he's smart, and maybe he is. Yet he's not the only one with skills."

They moved ahead again, walking toward the closest group of trees. It was hardly more than a handful, and the chance of an ambush inside it was remote, but it still took Faran all his courage to force himself to go beneath its canopy.

There was nothing there though, and it was pleasant inside it where the cold of the night still lingered.

"This will do nicely," Kareste said. "I would not do this out in the open where someone might be observing me."

"What will you do?" Faran asked

Kareste looked at him speculatively. "What *we* will do is spirit walk. In that way we can scout ahead and see if a trap is set for us."

Faran had heard of spirit walking before. At least, he understood the theory but it was not a magic that either Aranloth or Kareste had taught him.

"Is that not dangerous? Especially if we both go, there will be no one here to guard our bodies."

"You're right to be cautious. All magic has its dangers, and this one more than many. But it's a skill you may need in the future, and this is the best time to learn it. We're safe enough here, I think. At least for a short while. We must be swift."

Kareste sat down and leaned her back against a tree trunk. Faran did the same, looking across at her from a short distance. She considered him a moment, then spoke.

"This is how we'll do it. I'll let you join with me as I spirit walk. You'll see how it's done, and you'll be with me as I search. Yet at the same time, you'll still be here and watching over us just in case the enemy comes close. Does that make sense?"

Faran shook his head. "Not really."

"Never mind," Kareste replied. "This is one of those things that doing is far easier than trying to explain. Just follow along with what I say, and don't be afraid. That will hold us both back, and chain us to our bodies."

She relaxed then, breathing slowly. Her eyes were half lidded, and she seemed calm and tranquil.

Faran did the same. This was a kind of meditation, and he knew it well. His breathing was soft and slow, and he concentrated on the har-harat energy point just below his navel. He felt the warmth there straight away, sensed how energy circulated from there to the rest of his body. He was calm and at peace, and even the whisper of Kareste's voice within his own mind did not disturb him.

Can you hear me, Faran?

I hear you, he replied. This was much like the training they had once done with Aranloth where the lòhren had laid his mind over Faran's and Ferla's to teach them. But he sensed that Kareste did not have that skill, and her presence was barely there at all.

Join with me, she said faintly. *See through my eyes.*

Her voice was faint, but he sensed the origin of it, and he moved his concentration toward it, following it like he might follow the trail of an animal in the wilderness. She kept speaking, and he kept following.

Suddenly, his body felt lighter and with a lurch he realized his consciousness was in some part of her mind, and the world seemed to spin.

He looked out at her as she leaned against the tree, yet overlaying that was another image. He saw himself leaning against the trunk of a tree also, and the division of his senses like this made him feel nauseous.

Concentrate on what you see through my eyes, Kareste told him. *Do not seek to see both views at the same time.*

He did as she advised, and slowly his perception adjusted again. He looked out at the world through her eyes, and that was most of what he saw. His own view, through his own eyes, was become blurry and vague. Yet he could still see enough to tell if danger approached.

I'm ready, he told Kareste. *Let us spirit walk.*

He sensed her surprise at how quickly he had adjusted to this, and knew that their connection was stronger than just that of eyesight. He was in her mind, and the reactions and thoughts that she normally kept hidden were now more open to him.

This is the secret of the magic, she explained. *The flesh and the spirit are one, but they can draw apart. They do so in sleep. The body is heavy and cumbersome. The spirit is lighter than the wind. Feel the spirit rise up from the chains of the flesh and float free.*

Even as she spoke he felt a strange sensation. It was one of rising, like steam from boiling water, and suddenly he was with Kareste, floating in the air and looking down upon their still bodies below.

Just as in the void, Kareste said, *thought and action are one here. We can go where we will, and our thought makes it so.*

The world began to move slowly around them. It was a strange sensation, the strangest he had ever felt, but it was not unpleasant. Up they rose, and the small cluster of trees whirred around them, and then they were looking down on the trees from above. Kareste glanced around, searching all directions first, and he knew she was looking for any sign of the enemy approaching, but there was none.

We must be quick, she said, and he sensed her urgency.

The world moved again, and they sped northward toward the tombs, following the trail they would have walked. Yet they did so at great speed, fast as a hawk would fly, and once more Faran felt nauseous, and he sensed his body back among the trees.

Don't think of your body, Kareste warned. *That will only draw you back toward it and give you the sensations of the flesh. See with your eyes there but dimly, and concentrate on the here and now.*

The strange feeling subsided, and once more he enjoyed the sensation of flying. They sped ahead even faster.

They raced ahead, and then the ground rose up to meet them. They traversed a gully, wide and deep, in which the enemy could lie in wait. But there was nothing there but a muddy track at the bottom from the last fall of heavy rain. They rose up again out of that and sped toward another clump of trees.

This was a genuine wood, several acres in extent. Here, Kareste slowed and they wove through the aisles of trees, dim and shadowy.

It did not take them long to find what they sought, and even as Faran saw the enemy, he felt a sudden swell of emotion from Kareste. It was not fear, but it was deep concern. Almost, she had led them straight into a trap.

The trap was not quite what Faran had expected. They swung low, drifting among the lower branches of the trees and looked down at the enemy's camp. But it was not filled with soldiers from Faladir, nor even men.

It was a camp of elugs, and there were hundreds of them. They were creatures of legend. Goblins the old tales sometimes called them. Nearly as tall as a man, but strong and wiry. Their armor was poor, but their blades wickedly sharp and curved into crescents. They milled about, in the shadows, waiting.

How he knew, Faran was not sure. But these were elugs from the northern mountains rather than from the south. He realized that he had seen some banners they caried, and that they were a little taller than southern elugs. Then he realized this was not his knowledge at all but Kareste's.

The longer they were bonded this way by magic the closer their thoughts became.

Evil stirs, Kareste whispered in his mind. *Dark things gather to the call of the Morleth Stone, and creatures of the old world walk abroad in Alithoras.*

Faran felt her worry. *They serve the king now, and he gathers an army about him, does he not?*

Kareste glanced at the creatures below, and he felt memories rise of many battles against such things, then that thought was suppressed by Kareste and she answered.

It is the nature of evil. They must conquer and spread their taint everywhere. The king gathers an army, and he would become an emperor. Yet even in victory he would become, if he is not already, merely a slave.

Kareste had seen enough. She sped away then, flying like an arrow shot from a bow toward her body. The world flashed by, barely a blur, and then like falling from a great height Faran's spirit parted from her and entered his own body again.

It was a shock, and the heaviness of the flesh felt like chains about him. But in moments he readjusted. He looked over at Kareste. She was already standing, and he rose also, but he was unsteady on his feet.

"What now?" he asked.

She turned to him, and her grin was fierce. "Now we spring the trap set for us."

Faran was surprised. He had thought they would flee, trying to reach the tombs by circling far around.

"How can we spring the trap except by putting ourselves in danger?"

"Speed is our priority here, Faran. We must reach Aranloth swiftly, if it's not already too late."

"But how can we spring the trap, and survive?"

Kareste's grin only broadened, but he had never seen her look so fierce or determined.

"I have a plan," she answered. "But I won't say it isn't without danger."

4. A Shield of Thought

"What plan do you have?" Faran asked Kareste.

"I have skill with illusion. That you have seen for yourself. The Morleth Stone might bestow power on the knights, but it cannot give them experience to discern truth from misdirection. That is to our advantage."

They wasted no time after that, but headed out toward the trap that had been set for them. It seemed strange to Faran to walk over the country that he had flown over in spirit form only a short while since. Everything seemed different, and yet he could still recognize the landmarks that he had observed.

They crossed the long gulley that they had flown through, and then as the sun rose high in the wintery sky, they drew toward the larger wood wherein the elugs clustered.

"We will be seen and marked by now," Kareste observed.

Faran knew that was no idle bit of conversation. It was her warning to him that they had passed beyond the point of no return in this plan.

The land dropped a little again, though this was no gulley but merely a fold in the earth. Kareste must have noted it when they spirit walked though, and he felt sure that she had already planned ahead what they would do if a trap was set for them before they even discovered it.

The wood was lost from sight, and Kareste acted quickly. Halting, she raised her staff and created an image of herself. It was not done with the skill of the warriors Aranloth used to summon for the training of fighting skills, but it would certainly pass as real enough from a distance.

A moment later another form sprang up. It was Faran himself, and the image looked the real Faran up and down and shook his head as though in disgust.

Faran laughed, but he knew what Kareste was doing. This was her means of dissipating the tension that was building. Hopefully, her plan would work smoothly, but if it did not they now faced mortal danger. And just like Kubodin would make a joke in a situation like that, so too did Kareste. Battles of swords or of magic made no difference, for fear hindered people in any circumstances and it must be managed. Or it increased the risk of defeat.

With a flick of her staff the two figures began to move. They walked up the slope and into the view of the enemy. Indeed, they were walking straight toward them.

Kareste turned to him, and he saw the strain of concentration on her face.

"I'll need your help for the next bit," she said.

It was only then that Faran realized she intended to move out past the trap. He had expected that she would use it as a diversion and to swing out quite wide of the enemy.

His surprise must have shown because she gave him a tight grin.

"This really is the best way. I meant what I said that we cannot afford to waste time. Aranloth's life depends on it."

He nodded. "What can I do?"

"The illusions I just now created have to be good because the enemy will see them up close. But we need a cover as well, something to hide us from their eyes while they concentrate on the wrong thing."

He had seen her do this kind of thing before. "A mist then? Or maybe smoke?"

She shook her head. "Neither. They would be out of place here and just draw attention. That's not what we want. For this, we need something different, and you will have to do it. I'm already near my limits."

Again, she had caught him by surprise, but time was running out. Whatever they were to do, it must be done now, even if he did not think he had the skill.

"Show me what to do, and I'll try my best."

"Join minds with me Faran, as we did before to spirit walk. It will be easier to show you that way, and I might be able to add a few finer touches to the illusion you create."

He did as she asked, and he found he could do it swiftly this time. The bond they shared while spirit walking was still fresh, but now instead of him being drawn into her mind and seeing with her eyes, she overlayed her mind on his.

Think of aurochs came her voice, faintly but clearly as though it were one of his own thoughts.

They had seen several of the great beasts while they journeyed, and he pictured one now. It was a bull, and its great horns swept forward in graceful curves. He imagined the massive shaggy head, for the beasts now had their thick winter coat. Then he fixed in his mind the powerful body, the long tail swishing away flies and the thinner legs and hooves supporting it. He had seen that there was quite some variation in coloring, but he made this one a nondescript brindle color, which seemed to be the most common.

Very good, came Kareste's whisper in his mind. *Now invoke your magic. Pour it into the image like water from a jug into a cup and make the creature walk.*

It took some concentration, but he did what she said. It was often the case with magic that visualizing something made it reality, and her description of doing it like pouring water helped him understand how the magic worked.

Very good indeed, she said, and he sensed once more a little surprise at how quickly he had grasped what she had explained.

Now take that image, she instructed, *and replicate it. We need a herd of a dozen or so cows to hide behind.*

Faran was dumbfounded by such a request. It was all he could do to create one, and a dozen was surely beyond him. Yet still he made the attempt, and the strain of concentration was immense.

But the herd of cows appeared, even if some seemed blurry and obviously not quite right.

The enemy will see that this is an illusion, he said into Kareste's mind.

Perhaps. But their focus will be on my two figures, and a herd of aurochs moving naturally would seem blurred from a distance anyway as they move at different paces and one animal stands before another obscuring it. Just the movement alone will help hide any defects.

He did notice however that she poured just a little of her own magic into the illusions, and she made some of the animals appear bigger and others smaller so that the herd looked more natural.

We must move forward now, Kareste instructed. *Neither you nor I can keep these illusions intact for too long.*

They moved up the slope and out into the open. Ahead, and hundreds of feet to the right the illusions of himself and Kareste walked slowly toward the wood. They seemed perfectly lifelike to Faran, and they only served to make him worry how poor his own was.

Keep the aurochs between us and the wood like a shield, Faran.

He did as she said, but already the strain of concentration was wearing on him. But their lives might depend on this, for if the illusion faltered and they were seen they could not hope to defeat so many elugs.

34

They moved out into the open. Walking swiftly, they crossed the green grass in full view of the enemy. But Faran kept the herd between themselves and the wood, and at times he even made the herd jostle and trot a little so that they kept up with the fast pace that was being set.

In contrast, Kareste kept the illusion of the two of them walking at a slow pace, and now and then they turned toward each other and paused as though in conversation. But all the while those two illusions moved toward the right side of the wood, while Faran and Kareste themselves moved toward the left.

Sweat broke out on Faran's forehead, and he felt his concentration waver.

Hold steady, came Kareste's voice in his mind. She was calm and confident, and that eased his burden a little. He could do this. She would not have asked it of him unless she thought he could. He must endure.

Yet still, they were only halfway to the wood.

Faran stumbled ahead. How easy it was to wield a sword or swing an axe. But the weight of magic was heavier by far, and it wore him down. Yet still he maintained the illusion, and he and Kareste crossed the open ground with the herd of aurochs acting as a shield between them and the enemy.

Suddenly, there was a din of battle cries and wild shrieks and yells. The trap was sprung, and the elugs raced from the woods like maddened ants from a disturbed nest.

The elusions of Faran and Kareste turned away from the screaming horde and raced to the right. It was the opposite direction from the real quarry.

Faran stumbled and his concentration wavered. Partly from exhaustion but also from relief.

Do not waver! Came the command from Kareste. *Hold the illusion. We are not in the clear yet.*

It was true. There could still be lookouts left in the wood, and there had been no sign of Sofanil. Either when they spirit walked or now as his servants raced across the grass.

Where was he? Faran wanted to know, and he knew he would have felt much safer to see him chase Kareste's illusions. But there was no sign of him at all, and it was deeply troubling.

5. Days of Terror

It had been a cold night such as Faladir had rarely, if ever, endured.

Menendil had never experienced the like. All the hearths in the inn had fires lit, and yet still it was cold. He was wrapped in a bearskin cloak, and it was thick and heavy, yet it seemed small protection. That cloak had been handed down by his father, and the story that went with it was that his father had been attacked by a bear in the wild lands to the north and nearly mauled to death. But he had killed the bear with a spear.

It was an item of clothing that Menendil had rarely worn, but it was a regular addition to his clothing the last week.

For it had not just been a cold night, but a cold snap the like of which had folks muttering of a curse under their breath. No one in living memory had experienced anything like it. Water froze in jugs. Shallow wells had been rendered useless unless the layer of ice sealing them was broken. Birds had fallen dead into the street from buildings above, frozen. Trees in some of the parks had shattered, their trunks splitting with mighty cracks in the middle of the night. And some of the elderly, children and infirm had died in their sleep from cold and sickness.

The words *curse* and *evil* had been muttered many a time, at least when people still walked the streets. But it had been too cold for that lately. Even the markets opened only in the middle of the day, and but briefly, for few ventured out into the cold except those who had to.

Never before had the Bouncing Stone Inn had so few customers. That was saying something, for the last few months had been bad enough. But no one drank in the cold, and few came in for meals. In truth, it was only a handful of the poor that Menendil had been feeding, and there was no profit in that. He did it because his father had done it before him, and the inn was known to be a place where the desperate could find a meal and a bed to sleep in.

Menendil polished the old bar out of habit. It did not need it though. No beer had been spilled there for days. But it kept him active, otherwise he would merely shiver in bed until the midday sun had made life bearable.

He knew he should be grateful though. Cold as it was, and deadly as that was, it was not as bad as the morning of terror that had raged through the city after the Hundred had pulled down the statue of the king. That had been a week ago, and it unleashed horror enough to fill the nightmares of the insane.

The elù-draks had been loosed, and they had attacked in broad daylight. No one had been safe, and the streets had been filled with screams until all had found a building to enter and the doors and windows barred. Yet he had heard stories of the creatures descending chimneys into houses to murder those within. Whether that was true or not, he was not certain.

Elugs had been seen too. A company of goblins was said to have invaded one of the massive tenement buildings, five stories high, and to have cast out the occupants from the windows. Were-hounds had raced through the streets, baying and growling, and many were the doors with great grooves in them from the claws of the beasts as they tried to get inside. It had not happened at the inn, but Menendil had seen some of those marks on neighboring doors and they had made him shudder.

The cold, deadly as it was, was nothing compared to the terror of that morning. Yet there were those who said that the strange weather was a continuation of the terror brought down on the city by the curse of the king. Sorcery they called it, as evil as anything else that had happened.

Menendil had asked Caludreth about that, but the knight had shaken his head.

"I don't think so. The king is become a great sorcerer, stronger in magic by far than any of the knights, but the cold has lasted for days. He surely cannot have that power. I don't think even Osahka, whom the rest of the world knows as Aranloth, could do that. No. Set your mind at rest. This is natural."

Despite his own words, the knight had looked doubtful and gazed out the window with a creased forehead.

Menendil finished cleaning the bar. The inn was open, but there would be no customers. It did seem a little warmer though, and it was darker too. Clouds had drifted in during the morning.

He went to the door and opened it, looking out into the street. A blast of cold air came in, and the fire in the closest hearth leaped and twisted. He would not venture out into the street. It was empty as he thought it would be, yet the cold was not as great as he expected. He glanced up, and a gray sky looked back down at him, somber and grim with banks of clouds that seemed almost black.

There was nothing good to see, and he was about to close the door when he felt something on his arm. He was not sure at first, but then something struck his face. It was snow. Soon, there was a flurry of fat flakes drifting down and dusting the street.

This was new. This was the first good bit of news for days. For while snow was inconvenient, it meant the temperature must surely now warm a little. It always did when it snowed, and the cold spell would be broken. The clouds would trap a little of the warmth from the land, and the worst would be over.

He cried out in joy to the rooms above, for no one had ventured down here to the common room this morning.

"It's snowing!" he called, and he nearly laughed for the joy of it. "It's snowing, and it's wonderful!"

His wife was the first down, and she was shrugging on a heavy wool cloak as she walked. She shot him an annoyed glance, but her eyes widened as she looked outside.

"At last a bit of luck, Mender," she murmured. "Things will warm up now."

"That they will, Norla."

Caludreth came down the stairs with Norgril by his side. Norgril had been here on the morning of terror a week ago, and he had not left since. It had not been safe to do so, and Menendil was glad of the company anyway. And the extra sword if it came to that. Who knew what other terrors might be unleashed on the city next?

They both peered out the door in turn, and a flurry of wind blew some snowflakes across the threshold.

"Close the door!" Norla ordered. "We've all seen snow before, and that draught will bring illness with it. You can count on that."

Menendil complied, but he took one last long look at the snow before he did. It was marvelous to see, for there were winters in Faladir from time to time when no snow fell at all. But this was a different kind of winter, and even as he watched he saw that it began to fall even more heavily. He did not doubt that it would continue to do so, and that the depth of snow would be a record too.

He closed the door and went straight to the closest hearth. He stirred the fire a little, and added a new log. Keeping the door open had drained the room of warmth, and though the situation was improving it was still bitterly cold.

Caludreth did the same at another hearth, and the smell of smoke was stronger in the room. Menendil liked that, but he did worry if they had enough firewood. Yet there was a great pile stacked against the back wall of the inn, and that should see them out to the spring if they were careful. But they would have to be careful, for who knew when the timber carter would venture the streets again. For that matter, who knew if timber was even being cut outside the city walls. There had been no news from the outside world for over a week.

They sat down at the bar, and the room slowly began to lose some of its chill.

"I know just the thing to help warm us up," Menendil said, and he went around to the working side of the bar. He quickly found four glasses, small and well made. They were rarely used for customers unless Menendil was entertaining a noble or a merchant who was traveling and putting up his retinue in the inn. Customers such as those got the little luxuries such as he was about to make.

He took an earthenware mug as well, far larger than the glasses, and from a bottle kept beneath the bar he poured some spirit into the mug. He never served this to regular customers because it was expensive, and he acquired only a few bottles a year from a friend. But it was powerful and felt like fire when he drank it.

Diluting the mix with red wine, again something rarely drunk in his inn, he then mixed in some spices and a few spoons of honey.

Norla watched him with a frown. She knew what he was making and she had seen him get drunk on it before, but he had learned since then to only enjoy the brew in small quantities. The others had never seen it before and watched with curiosity.

41

Their curiosity was only increased when he did not serve it straight away but instead took the mug to the hearth and placed it among the coals.

"A lot of trouble for a small drink," Norgril observed.

It was not the first time Menendil had heard that. The merchants often said the same thing, though the better-traveled ones knew what he was doing, and their eyes gleamed in appreciation.

"You'll learn," was all Menendil said in reply.

"Aye," his wife added. "You'll learn, but only the one batch, Mender. No more than that."

Norla knew how strong this stuff was too, and he remembered well how she served it up to a merchant on a cold morning last winter before they negotiated the price to be paid for his retinue staying two days and his horses to be fed and cared for.

He used the bar cloth to hold the hot mug when the drink was ready, and he poured it into the glasses on the bar. The sweet and spicy smell of the drink filled the air, and the others grew interested. This was like nothing they had seen before.

They sipped their drinks quietly while the room warmed. Diluted as it was, and sweetened by the honey, Mender still felt the fire of it in the pit of his stomach.

"Remarkable," Caludreth said.

"Quite!" Norgril agreed.

Menendil ginned at them, and took another sip himself.

The world outside was hushed, but he glanced through the window and saw that the snow was falling thickly now. It showed no sign of letting up. There was still a sense of doom, of winter actually trying to kill them, but the warm glow of the drink was beginning to take the edge off that.

"You know what we need now?" Norla said. "We need a story. On days like this my dad used to tell my sister and me stories. That's what we need to pass the time."

6. Conlar and Cerwen

Menendil remembered his own father telling stories in this very room long ago, and he knew it was part of the training of the knights, so he turned to Caludreth.

The once-knight sat back in his chair and thought. Outside, a wind began to howl and the snow pummeled against the window. If things kept up as they were, the streets would be deep in snow within hours, and if there had been little chance of customers before there would be none then.

"Very well. This is one of the old tales, handed down from a time just after the end of the elù-haraken. We all know the stories of the first king, and how he, his army, and Aranloth broke the siege of Faladir and captured the Morleth Stone. But did you know the king had a younger brother?"

The others shook their heads. They did not know, but Menendil knew this tale, and it was indeed old. Both in terms of when the events took place and also in terms of when he had last heard it. His father had told him the story once when he was a child, but it was long ago and half forgotten.

"This is the tale of Conlar and Cerwen," the once-knight said. His voice had taken on a deeper pitch, and it was slower and smoother than his usual manner of speaking.

"It is a story of hope and love, and the fight against the dark forces of the world. That is most fitting to hear now, but there is never a time when it is not."

Menendil took a sip of his drink and felt warmth creep through him. Just now, he cared nothing that there were no customers and that he was idle at a time when the inn should be busy coming up to lunch.

"Of old," Caludreth went on, "just after the end of the Shadow Wars, Conlar was still eager for adventure. He was young and strong, and he had no family and thirsted for adventure. So too, despite the great victory his brother had won, there still existed pockets of evil in the world. So it was that Conlar left Faladir, and with him went his trusted retinue and hundreds of soldiers. They thirsted for adventure, and they took it as a personal affront that evil still existed in the realm, no matter that there were only small enclaves and they had gone into hiding on the high ridges and in the deep valleys."

Menendil half closed his eyes, but he did not feel sleepy. Rather, he listened with great attentiveness, and despite that he could almost believe his own father was here telling this story once more. All the knights adopted a similar way of talking, formal and slow and solemn when they told a story. It was the way Osahka trained them.

"Conlar traveled widely, and he rooted out the remnants of evil that still dwelled in the land. Some fled before his wrath, but others fought back because his force was not large. Many were the pitched battles that were fought, but at great risk to himself and through the bravery of those he led, they prevailed.

"So it was that he opened up the land, and hardy farmers followed after him, and they tilled the earth and raised livestock. Many things they grew also, from vines to fruit trees to grains, and they prospered. So also they built homesteads, and eventually married and raised families under the peace that Conlar had established.

"But Conlar himself did not marry. He moved on, and ever he walked toward danger. When rumor came to him

45

of some other stronghold of evil, thither he went with his soldiers and there they faced danger again. It was no way to live, and no circumstance under which to place a wife or raise children. But it is said that he was lonely and envied the farmers who married in the lands he had cleansed and prospered with wives and children.

"The years wore on, and Conlar eventually tired of battle and bloodshed. So it was that after purging one more valley he rested a while, and a while became longer, and he found the valley fair and felt no desire to leave it.

"That valley he called Dromdruin, and there was a creek that ran through it and fair woods, ancient and majestic, on the lower slopes. But to the north, on a high ridge, there he and his men raised a manor house, and he asked for builders from the city which his brother the king gladly sent to him, and they crafted a dwelling of great beauty, but also fortified, for he mistrusted the evils of the world and though it was a safer place because of him it was still not *entirely* safe.

"Around that manor house a village sprang up, and the soldiers dwelled there also, but soon they spread out onto the lower slopes where the soil was more fertile and they established farms."

Caludreth looked at them then, and with a sigh he broke his story.

"I have been to that manor house, or what is left of it. They are only ruins now, and the ancient forest has reclaimed what once was its own. Long years have passed, and the world has changed. But it is always said that Conlar was happy there."

Menendil did not like that the manor house and village were gone. But it was the way of the world. Nothing lasted forever, and it often seemed the good things failed to endure and the lesser lasted longer. But the valley itself still endured, and the descendants of the brave folks who settled there lived on. Their blood was the blood of heroes, and that was a testament that lasted longer than things constructed of wood or even stone.

"Conlar at last sought peace," Caludreth continued, "but trouble and battle came to him instead, and unexpectedly.

"Out of the wild lands to the north that he and his soldiers had not yet cleansed with their swords, came a horde of elugs. Dark things yet lived, just as they do now, and they rise up from time to time. This is the cycle of life in Alithoras. Neither the Light nor the Dark has ever yet gained total supremacy.

"The elugs raided and slew, and many were the homesteads burned down and the fields trampled that once grew wheat. And those fields were watered by blood, and swift word came to the manor house.

"Conlar donned his armor once more, and wrath was in his eyes and a cold fire burned the length of his sword. In fury he marched from his abode with his retinue that lived there, and as he traveled he gathered survivors about him. On they marched, following the trail of the elugs.

"The trail was plain to see. Death and destruction marked it, and Conlar knew a towering rage for all the slain and the good things they had wrought that now lay charred and smoking beneath the roof of the forest. Even some of the forest itself burned, and whether that was by chance or design of the elugs, none knew. Yet it slowed down the pursuit.

"On the second day of the march, Conlar was forced to go wide of a great blaze and he lost the trail of the enemy. But he called to him Cerwen, a hunter and tracker in his retinue that had joined but recently, and he gave her the task of finding the trail once more.

"This she did, for she was skilled. The enemy had veered to the east, and they had descended a rocky slope whence smoke from the fires was being blown. So they had hoped to escape, but they counted not on Cerwen's skill nor her fervor for the chase. For she hated elugs with a passion. They had killed her seven brothers at the breaking of the siege of Faladir.

"Conlar gained on the enemy, and his wrath gave him strength and the anger of his followers sped their march. They closed on the enemy as the sun dipped downward bringing on afternoon. But not all was as it seemed, and the air was still filled with smoke making it hard to see.

"Again, by chance or design, the elugs being pursued joined forces with another group of their brethren. Now they far outnumbered those who would bring them the justice of the sword, and they turned and held their ground.

"But Conlar attacked, unaware of their greater numbers until too late, and battle was joined in fury. The soldiers of Faladir were veteran fighters, and they fought for their home and the sake of loved ones murdered, yet they were outnumbered too heavily.

"The soldiers of Faladir fell in great number, and Conlar ordered a retreat so that some at least could escape. To help them, he and a small number of his retinue charged the enemy.

"This tactic worked, and a few escaped, fleeing back into the smoke as afternoon fell. But the brave retinue of Conlar was slain. Conlar himself, badly wounded, fought on, and it is said that he killed many of the enemy by himself before he fell.

"But he was not killed. Rather he was stunned by a blow to the back of his helm and he was taken prisoner instead. At this, the elugs rejoiced, for they were vicious and gave no quarter to foes. Better for them to have a live enemy and entertain themselves by his slow killing, and all the more so for they knew who Conlar was. There would be no mercy, and the death promised him was bitter.

"As night fell, he was taken to a tree and there tied. The elugs held a ceremony, ancient and evil, and they heated their knives in their campfires and sang to the dark sky while their excitement built.

"Then they plied their trade of terror. At first, Conlar made no sound. Then he cursed his enemies. At the last, he cried his anguish to the same dark skies. But no tale tells that he ever begged for mercy.

"The elugs relented. Not out of mercy, for they had none. But their sport was lessened when Conlar fainted and could not be revived. So too, the night had grown old and the tiredness of battle wore on them. They set guards and slept, and they did so in peace for the next morning they would begin again on their great enemy and there were no foes nearby to harass them.

"But they were wrong. Cerwen had retreated at the order, but when she realized what Conlar had done and how he had bought the lives of the few who had escaped with his own, she knew great anguish.

"She was alone. Yet even so she doubled back to discover the fate of her leader, and when she read the tracks and realized he was taken prisoner she knew what that meant, and her anguish increased.

"Yet she was no fainthearted hunter. A hero's soul dwelled in her, and her heart beat with courage. She could not save Conlar, yet she vowed to herself in the dark reaches of that terrible night that she would end Conlar's torment. A single arrow would do it, and it would be a mercy to him.

"Tears in her eyes, Cerwen crept through the ring of sentries the elugs had thrown up to protect their camp a mile to the north. Her bow she carried, and it was strung, but no arrow notched yet. If she were discovered, she

49

would suffer the same fate as Conlar. So instead she held a knife in her other hand, the blade covered with dirt to help hide the glint of steel in the night. With this, she would end her own life rather than be taken alive.

"And so, she crept forward as the night wore on, and entered the sprawling camp of the enemy and passed ever so slowly through the sleeping forms, crawling on the ground and relying on the dark, her skill, and most of all on luck to hide her.

"Conlar stirred, waking from his slumber that shielded him from pain, and he moaned softly. At this Cerwen stilled, for should he cry out and waken the enemy they might commence again their torture. If so, she would be discovered.

"The night grew cold, and Cerwen shivered. She felt fear such as she had never known, and she cursed herself for a fool. Why was she here? Why had she come so deep into the camp when she could have loosed an arrow from closer to its perimeter and had some chance of escape? That was what she had planned for.

"Conlar raised his head slowly, and she was close enough now to see his face. Even in the dim light she saw the blood that marred it. So too his shirt had been torn and drenched where he had bled from a hundred cuts. Conlar saw her, and his eyes widened. His body was broken, but his mind was still his own, and he made no sound that would draw attention to her, but with his eyes he indicated she should flee.

"So it was that she realized why she had come here. He was a man who put the safety of others before his own. He was a hero in a group of hard men, heroes all themselves. She had not come to put him out of his misery and spare him worse to come. She had crept through the camp to rescue him.

"Cerwen looked at him no more, lest her heart break for pity. Instead, she kept crawling, and every move made her fear discovery. Yet at length she came up behind the tree, and there she stood. Slowly, carefully, gazing round her at the enemy that surrounded her, she cut the ropes that bound Conlar to the tree.

"When the last of the ropes severed, he nearly fell, but her arm went around him and supported him.

'Can you walk?' she whispered.

'I can try,' came his answer, and his voice was soft but roughened with pain.

"She slipped the handle of her knife into his hand, and he knew what it was for. Not defense, but to kill himself if they were discovered, and she drew another knife for herself. For how could they not be discovered? If Conlar tried to crawl, he might never get up again. The wounds to his chest would also be opened up and cause debilitating pain. Yet how could they hope to walk out of the camp of their enemies? Even now, not all the elugs were asleep and it would only take one suspicious glance to give them away. Or one glance at the tree where their captive was no longer tied.

"But her arm around him, she supported him as they began to shuffle toward escape. Several times, she knew they were seen. An elug stirred, looking up at her. Another one muttered, half sitting up and clutching his side. He had been wounded in the previous battle. Yet despite the cold shiver of fear that ran through her, no one raised an alarm. They were, perhaps, taken to be two more wounded elugs themselves in the dark.

"Conlar was a man of courage and strength. Sensing the possibility of freedom, and now moving more freely as his stiff limbs began to loosen up, she needed to support him less.

"At just that moment though, a cry went up. Several elugs sprang up toward the tree where Conlar had been tied, and they drew their swords and shouted.

"All around them the camp roused to life, and elugs stumbled up drawing their weapons. Where before soldiers were asleep, now the world boiled to life.

"In the midst of this, Conlar and Cerwen pretended to be just two more elugs. And by destiny, or luck, or some twist of fate they reached the edge of the camp before they were discovered. There Conlar turned and slashed the throat of an elug who had flung out a hand to stop him. The elug died, and a warning went up from several throats, but Cerwen was already leading Conlar into the night and they raced away under cover of darkness.

"A hue and cry rose up all about them, and Cerwen knew her charge could not run far. But they did not have to. Deeper into the valley she led him, but even as they came to the bottom he faltered.

'Flee!' Conlar commanded.

'Never!' she replied, and she was heartened by the sound of the creek that rushed and bubbled nearby.

"She grabbed him, half carrying him down toward the edge of the water. There, among the reeds, she found the crude raft she had made before striking out toward the elug camp. It was little more than a group of saplings bound together by vines, and she was not sure if it would support the weight of two people.

"They pushed it out into the water, and it floated. Then Conlar staggered and fell upon it, and Cerwen lay down upon him and held on as the current of the creek took them.

"But the elugs came upon them, and they cast spears at them, but missed for the darkness that swallowed them and the speed of the water that took them. Yet even as they floated toward safety, an elug archer, by luck or skill, sped an arrow into Cerwen's back. She cried out, and the elugs jeered, then she lost consciousness.

"They escaped, though the elugs tried to find them for a while, running by the creek bank. But they had no desire to tarry for they did not know if reinforcements might arrive with the new day that was now not far off. So it was that by mid-morning, free of the enemy but fearing for Cerwen's life, Conlar tended her. He carried her, despite the pain of his wounds, to a cave that he knew. Her wound was deep, and her red blood flowed like the long red hair that tumbled down her back. In the cave, he drew out the arrow and gave her such healing as he could. Over time, he brought her back to health, and ragged and weary eventually returned to his home.

"Great was the surprise of his people, and great their rejoicing. Yet this grew greater still when he announced Cerwen had consented to wed him.

"In due course, the two heroes were married, and it is said they both lived long and happy lives afterward, each deeply in love with the other, and that they raised a large family. But Dromdruin never fully recovered from the raid, and the population remained sparse and eventually only the farmers remained and generations after Conlar and Cerwen the old manor was abandoned and the forest reclaimed it.

"So ends the tale of Conlar and Cerwen," Caludreth said, and there was a gleam of emotion in his eyes as he finished.

7. Only Time will Tell

Faran at last let the illusion of aurochs that he maintained falter. He and Kareste had now gone past the edge of the wood where the trap had been set for them, and there was little chance of being seen.

He fell to the ground, exhausted.

Kareste seemed tired also, but only a little. That, he realized, was another kind of illusion itself. She would be as tired as he was, for she had done the same thing. But she was a lòhren, and she did not show it.

She knelt beside him. "You did well. There are lòhrens who would struggle to do what you have just done, though they are older and more experienced."

That was reassuring, but he still felt weak and he feared that should some new problem beset them he would be unable to counter it.

"Are your illusions still misleading the enemy."

She grinned at him, and suddenly did not look even a little tired.

"They are, but they don't exist anymore. I made them drop low into tall grass, and it would appear to the elugs that they have somehow hidden from sight. We can only hope the enemy spends hours scouring the countryside where they were last seen."

Faran was too tired to laugh, but he did anyway. Then he put his head in his hands and took a few deep breaths. Looking up again, he asked the question he feared having an answer to.

"There was no sign of Sofanil. Where do you think he is?"

That removed the last traces of her humor. "I wish I knew. Truly, I do. I'll not feel safe until I reach the tombs. Sofanil is a canny opponent, and I won't underestimate him."

They rested briefly, but within the span of minutes they were walking again. They kept a close watch all around them, but especially behind. The elugs had been fooled, but that could not be expected to last forever. At some point, either slowly or swiftly, they would realize they had been duped. Illusions left no tracks.

"Have you considered," Faran asked as they walked, "that Sofanil is somewhere ahead of us? Perhaps there is another trap?"

"I have considered that, yes. And we must be wary of such a thing. But I'm not sure if he has enough elugs or soldiers from Faladir to divide his forces so much. More likely, we have fooled him, and he is behind us. But not for long, I fear."

"Perhaps," Faran countered, "we haven't fooled him, and he's just being cautious. He might be watching us now with another group of elugs."

Kareste gave a slight shrug. "Maybe. We cannot know for sure. This much we can be certain of though. Sofanil is clever, and he must have learned by now that Lindercroft is dead. Both of those things *would* make him cautious. But none of the knights lack courage, so if he is out there, we'll see him soon."

They traveled warily, continuing as they had done before. It seemed to Faran now that he had spent his life like this, and he missed the old days where he could walk a forest trail or cross a meadow with nothing to fear but that he might scare game.

But his life had changed, and there was no going back. He could never go back. Even if it were safe for him to return to Dromdruin, that home would never be home to him again. Too much had changed, and too many memories haunted him.

All this way of thinking, and the constant fear, made Faran uneasy. He wanted to string his bow, but he resisted that urge. He would have time enough, he hoped, if a problem arose.

They pushed ahead at speed. The afternoon shadows grew long, and then dusk settled over the land. The two of them were like shadows themselves, fleeting over the country, lingering nowhere and as ephemeral as the dappled light itself.

After a while, Kareste changed direction slightly. She veered a little to the west, and Faran knew why. If Sofanil was still ahead of them she did not want to repeat the mistake they had made earlier of going in the same direction all the time. That made them predictable and vulnerable to another ambush. But it brought a problem with it too.

"This path will take us farther away from the entrance to the tombs," he said.

She grinned at him. "It takes us farther away from the entrance that *you* know. But the tombs are vast and mysterious. There are many entrances, some obvious and some hidden. Even I don't know them all, but the building near the waterfalls is far from the only way in or out."

That was a little surprising, but it made sense. The ancient Letharn had no need to limit the entrances in order to better guard them. The harakgar were there for that.

"What will we have to do when we get there?" he asked. "I mean for Aranloth."

She did not look at him, but kept her gaze on the land ahead that was now full of night shadows.

"Time will tell," she replied quietly, and kept walking.

56

There was something in her answer that worried Faran. He knew her well now, and he trusted her with his life. Yet he knew instinctively that she was holding something back.

8. The Shadow's Own Luck

Faran and Kareste moved ahead into the dark, but they slowed. Haste was necessary, but caution might save their lives.

The grass became dewy, and the stars glittered coldly in the sky. From the west, a slight breeze blew briefly, and then died away leaving the world still and silent.

About them, the land slowly changed. The slopes were longer and less steep, but there was a sense of moving downhill more often than not. They were approaching the Carist Nien, the river that split in two to form the Angle where the heartland of the Letharn Empire of old had lain.

They approached a gulley. A long while Kareste stood before it, unmoving. Something had triggered her instincts, but then she gave another of those slight shrugs she so often did and Faran followed her down the slope.

She moved slowly though. Whether this was still caution, or just the steepness of the ground, Faran did not know. But he had trouble keeping upright himself. The slope was steep, and the dewy grass made it dangerous.

At the bottom of the gulley Kareste began to walk its length rather than climb up the other side. This was likely an attempt to slow down any pursuit. At least Faran thought so. Just as they were nervous of an ambush now, so too might anyone be who followed them. That would slow them down.

They had not gone far though before Kareste stopped once again. She did not move, and Faran did not speak. He trusted her instincts for they were better than his own. Then she did something that surprised him.

Slowly, she raised her staff, and then a faint light pulsed from it. It was no stronger than moonlight on a full moon, but they could see by it.

This was a dangerous thing to do. These were wild lands, and a light such as this, though not strong, might be seen for miles all around. It could give them away. That they were in a gulley offered them some concealment, but the glow of light would still rise upward.

Kareste hissed softly, and at first Faran did not know why. Then he saw. The dewy grass ahead of them was marked by tracks. Many of them. Beyond, the bottom of the gulley was choked by bushes and shrubs. No water had flowed through here for long years, and there was likely no water to drink. So there was small chance that the tracks belonged to a herd of animals.

Even as Faran realized all this, there was a rush of movement from amid the cover ahead.

A horde of elugs poured out, shrieking fiercely and drawing their crescent swords, and with them this time was an enemy greater still. Sofanil himself was there, and he seemed calm and serene among the turmoil of his servants, but all the more determined than they to bring death and destruction.

Kareste reacted quickly. A moment she stood, transfixed by the surprise of seeing her enemy and the chagrin that he had not been fooled earlier, but then she acted.

With a decisive move she raised high her staff. A peel of thunder sounded, and the earth reverberated with it. The elugs paused, uncertain, then a gale of sudden wind drove down the gulley, and the scent of rain was on it.

"Run!" she cried at Faran, and they sped off. They did not go back up the gulley the way they had come, but rather she led him straight up the bank to the side.

Faran feared the enemy would be right behind him, but when he glanced over his shoulder to look they were not. Instead, they were running back the direction they had come.

He was not sure why, but then he caught sight of a towering wall of water that raced down the gulley. White froth topped it, and it roared as it tumbled forward uprooting shrubs. Debris roiled with it, and lightning flashed above.

Atop the gulley at each side, outlined by the flickering light that tore the sky, stood two elùgroths, their wychwood staffs held high. The elugs screamed in fear. They served elùgroths, but these two appeared to have summoned the lightning, and it flashed from the heavens to the tips of their staffs, and then these were lowered to point in the gulley.

Faran scrambled to the top and raced out over the grass, following Kareste. He had thought he could run fast, but the armor slowed him and she was swifter than he could ever imagine.

She sensed that he was falling back, and slowed slightly. But Faran had found his rhythm now, and he ran with the long stride that he had used so often in Dromdruin to cover the miles. It was not his fastest pace, but it was quick, and he could run like that for a long time.

He did not look back. The enemy would soon regroup and commit to the chase. There had been no wall of water in the gulley. Nor thunder and lightning. Neither had there been twin elùgroths bringing down vengeance on the elugs who served but feared them. It had all been illusion, he realized, and they would not be deceived for long. Not long at all, but whatever time Kareste had bought with her magic, she and Faran must use now to their best advantage. If they could get far enough away the night would hide them, and the enemy would have a much harder time trying to find them.

They ran ahead, and there was noise behind them of a pursuit. Elugs cried out, and there were answering shouts in a wide arc spreading out behind. Faran glanced momentarily over his shoulder, but despite how close the noise sounded he could see nothing.

Kareste veered a little to the left. Faran thought for a moment she was just trying to move in an unpredictable course, but then he saw that they were headed for a wood. It did not look large, but it was hard to tell. The trees bulked up before them, tall and shadowy.

There would be no safety in there. But there was less out in the open lands, and Faran did not hesitate to follow the lòhren as she sprinted for it.

A canopy of darkness fell over them as they entered the forest. The trees were mostly oaks, and it was an old wood, the trunks gnarled and rough, the litter of leaves on the ground deep and thick.

They slowed down. It was hard to see anything at all, and they could not run here. The pursuit behind them had faded away, for the enemy had not changed direction, but soon they would see the trees and reason that the wood offered cover. They would search here soon enough.

"Damn that Sofanil," Kareste cursed under her breath. "He set *two* traps for us."

"But how did he know to place it where he did?" Faran asked.

"He has the Shadow's very own luck," she said moodily. "That is all. He guessed, but he guessed wisely."

They had not gone much farther when a din sounded behind them again. The elugs were in the wood, and then there was a flair of light as they lit torches before it faded away as they headed in a slightly different direction.

"What now?" Faran whispered. He was surprised that he remained calm and spoke evenly.

Kareste gave no answer, and he was not sure if there was one to give.

9. That Look in Your Eye

The snow fell. And it kept on falling.

Menendil had never seen the like before. Nor had Faladir. The city streets were deep with it. Doors were shut hard, and impossible to open for the white banks piled against them. Roofs groaned with the weight of it. The air seemed filled for days on end with the driving assault of it, or a feather-light drifting. Or anything between.

But it kept snowing. And the world seemed silent except for the wind that at times swept through the city.

It was an eerie feeling to sit in the common room of the Bouncing Stone and to hear no people nor see anything from the windows. It was like being in the wild and isolated from the rest of the world despite being in a city that once teemed with people, noise, traffic and celebrations.

But at least the great cold had died away. It was merely cold, and Menendil could live with that.

So it went from one day to the next. Then from one week to the next. Yet the time came when the skies cleared and the sun shone once more. That was like a warm meal to a starving man, and at last there were signs of life.

People walked the streets, even if they were deep in snow and it was a struggle. Doors were opened and the drifts that held some fast were cleared away by strangers. Menendil had been forced though to exit by the back door to the inn, with a shovel, and make his way to the front. What once had been a journey of mere moments had taken minutes, for the snow was deep down the east side of the inn, but he cleared the front eventually.

The bench near the door was not visible, for it was buried deep. To that, he paid no heed. He loved to sit there of a morning, but that pleasure would have to wait. He had other jobs that needed doing.

People would be hungry, and he knew it. Their stores would be low for few would have been able to reach the markets and there would have been little produce there anyway. But the inn held good reserves of cured meats and sausages. Not to mention flour for the making of bread. Folks would be coming here to eat, and he and Norla were getting ready for that.

It was not just for warm food that they would come. They had been locked away in their own homes and secluded. They would hunger for news too, and for talk with other people.

Menendil expected the inn to get busy, and he was not disappointed. Through the day a stream of people came in, mostly folks who were looking for that warm meal and a chance to talk and swap stories. These were generally regular customers that he knew from days before things had turned bad in the city. They were all smiles and there was joy and laughter, but at times there was a haunted look to their eyes as they whispered something to a close friend they trusted.

No one in the city had escaped unscathed from the morning of terror and the cold that had descended afterward. Everyone knew someone who had died, whether it was from cold or something else. There were disappearances too. Some folks had vanished without trace, and though these were assumed to be dead too, no one really knew and that was perhaps even more unnerving.

Toward dusk the door opened and an older man came in. Menendil knew his type instantly. He was wealthy, but he made no great show of it. His clothes were nice and fashionable, but not luxuriant. His gaze took in the room and customers, and assessed everything with experienced judgement.

Menendil gave him a slight bow. This man was a merchant, and that might mean good busines.

"How can I help, good sir," Menendil greeted him.

"Have you rooms to spare? Ten of them?"

Menendil had more than ten rooms, and all were empty, yet still he scratched his head and looked thoughtful.

"I believe so," he answered after a moment. "I think we can find that much space."

The merchant did not grin, but the corners of his mouth twitched ever so slightly. He was indeed a man of experience, and he knew how this game was played.

"I'm Grundar, a grain merchant," he stuck out his hand and Mender shook it.

The merchant had a grip strong as iron, and Menendil reassessed him. He was a merchant now, but he had risen to that status. He had started life as a laborer of some kind. Both his grip and his unpretentious manner announced that.

They discussed a price for the night, and the rest of the merchant's team came inside. Mostly, they were guards. Hard men by their eyes, and their hands did not stray far from their swords. But though they were watchful and alert, they did not look in the least like the type to cause trouble. They would have a hot meal, a drink or two and then go to bed. There would be no carousing from them, and that was something Menendil preferred. Drunk men and swords were not a good match.

Norla took one of Grundar's men up to look at the rooms, and he gave a nod to his employer when he came back that all was well. They quickly arrived at a price for stabling and feeding their horses too, and bringing three caravans in around the back. Menendil steeply discounted that, for he had no staff yet to look after the livestock.

Grundar took that in his stride. He had obviously been in the city long enough to understand why the usual staff at an establishment like this were not there.

The evening passed pleasantly. Norgril came down for dinner, but Caludreth kept himself scarce. The guests of the inn were not locals, but one never knew. There could be a spy among them, and Caludreth's description was well circulated. He did not miss out though. Norla took both beer and food to his room, and she stayed there too to keep conversation with him. No guest had ever been treated better, and of anyone else Menendil would be jealous. But the knights had once been held in tremendous esteem in Faladir, and he was treated here as once any of the knights would have been treated anywhere in the realm, and sometimes beyond.

Grundar was a softly spoken man, but he was shrewd and well-mannered. As the night grew old his tongue loosened a little, and he told stories of some of his journeys around Alithoras. At times one of his guards sang, too. This man was blond haired and he did not have the look about him of Faladir at all. He sang with a deep, booming voice and the ballads he chanted were ones Menendil had never heard before. They woke in him a longing to see other lands and to venture wide across the vast stretches of Alithoras. What lands were there that he had never trod? What people whom he had never met?

Most of the guards drifted upstairs to their rooms where they bunked two to three together on the narrow but comfortable beds Mender provided. But Grundar seemed one of those who enjoyed late nights and late risings, at least when he was not on the road.

The merchant and his few remaining guards shifted to a table near the hearth in the far wall. The night was growing cold, and drinking beer only made that worse. However, they much approved of Menendil's brew, and called it the best they had drunk all year.

They called for more drinks, and Menendil went down to the cellar with the jug. He filled it with his best beer, and came back up and expertly filled their mugs with the liquid gold.

"Come join us for a drink, Mender," the merchant invited. "You're a fine host, and we like your company."

Mender gave a bow. "I'm most obliged, and truth be told I'm partial to a drink before going to bed myself."

"Aye," Grundar replied, "a publican who doesn't drink his own beer is worrisome. If he doesn't like it, then why should his guests?"

There was truth in that, and Menendil had learned from very early on that the best way to sell beer was to drink some in front of his customers who had only come in for a meal. He did not try to convince them to try any, but he smiled as he drank and he drank quickly like a man greatly enjoying it.

They sat for a while and talked quietly. Menendil learned that his first guess about the merchant had indeed been correct. He had started as a laborer, more specifically a farmer. His firm handshake had been proof of that, for the man had grown up milking cows. But he had moved on from dairying to buy the neighbor's farm, and grain was grown there. He had had successive years of good crops, and purchased other farms until soon he had a large business running. Then he had moved into transporting and selling the grain himself, cutting out the agents. He still owned all the land he had started with, and more besides, but he found he preferred the role of merchant where he crossed the land and met new people all the time. And he had granaries across many farms where he stored grain in anticipation of higher prices.

Norgril joined them at the table having come from upstairs. He had not said what he was doing, but no doubt he had been talking to Caludreth and letting him know that all was well down here and that there was no indication of spies from the king being in this group.

"I expect," Menendil commented, "that the price of grain in Faladir has risen over winter. I'm surprised though that you managed to travel here, given the weather. Faladir has never seen anything like this."

Grundar grew silent and thoughtful. He took a slow sip of the beer before he answered.

"A strange thing, that is. Certainly, the price has been … favorable."

Menendil understood his hesitation there. Most likely he had received a tremendous price for his grain. Food in the city was growing short, but it was not wise to advertise that he had profited well. But Menendil was in business himself and did not begrudge him that. The quest for profit was the mother of innovation and hard work. Those who received it earned it by their labor and risk. Those who did not strive through hard work toward profit expected others to shoulder their own burden.

"This cold you have here," Grundar continued, "and most likely the snow itself is a strange thing. A hundred miles away the weather is much more pleasant. It was only on approaching the city that the weather changed, and I had heard that from another merchant who I chanced to meet with on the road. I had not wanted to come here at all."

The man had not said why, but Menendil knew. Rumors of the goings on in this city must have spread far and wide, but it was still surprising to learn that the weather here was isolated to close around the city. Again he wondered if this was a curse from the king, but it was not a line of thought that he liked.

He changed the subject and asked another question. It was innocent enough, but as soon as he heard the answer he knew his life had taken another twist.

"Who bought the grain?"

Grundar looked troubled at this, and it was the first time that he had been ill at ease. Perhaps, without a few drinks to loosen his tongue, he might never have spoken at all.

"The king purchased it, and he did not mind the price either. He has money to spend, that one."

"The king?" replied Menendil. "Do you think he is going to distribute flour through the city? Many folks have been going hungry, lately."

The merchant gave a single but definitive shake of his head.

"I don't think so. The rumor is that he's building his army. The city folk might grow hungry, but not his soldiers."

This had indeed been Menendil's guess, but when looking for information in a way that seemed innocent it was better to say something and be corrected than to ask directly.

But he did ask the next question directly. "Where is the grain now?"

Even as he asked that he saw Norgril look at him intently. He knew why the question was asked, but then he looked away as though indifferent.

"We unloaded in the warehouses in the north of the city, up behind the palace."

Menendil asked nothing else. He knew that district, and where the warehouses were. The merchant went off to his room after that; he could afford one all to himself, and the remainder of his men went with him.

Norgril took a sip of beer from his mug, and spoke softly into the now silent room.

"I see that look in your eye, Mender."

Menendil looked away. Sometimes, he wished he was only an innkeeper and not the leader of the Hundred.

10. Hunted Like Prey

Kareste led Faran forward, and they moved like wraiths through the wood.

Faran was a hunter, and he had spent years learning how to move silently and invisibly in all sorts of terrain. From Dromdruin, only Ferla was his match. Yet Kareste amazed him. She was better than he was, able to move more silently than he, and at a faster pace. In fact, he realized that she had slowed down in order for him to keep pace with her.

The wood was an old one, and there was little undergrowth. The roof of boughs above prevented most sunlight penetrating to the forest floor, and now, at night, it was dark as the pit. A faint glow burgeoned from the tip of Kareste's staff. It was softer than moonlight, but it enabled them to see.

Despite the darkness in the wood, they needed something more to hide them. They needed cover, for their pursuers had lit torches.

All around now, sometimes distant and at other times closer to hand, there was a tumult of elugs. They cried out and yelled. They beat their way through the wood, trampling through the leaf litter, skidding down slopes, hacking at low branches with their swords. They had no woodcraft at all, but what they lacked in skill they made up for in numbers.

Faran knew there was no hiding from them. At any moment they might be spied, and then the cry and hunt would begin. Perhaps there were elugs on the grasslands searching too, for he and Kareste had not been seen and the enemy could not know for sure where they were, but the wood was a better guess, and the elugs seemed to have confidence in that.

Kareste veered to the left. Here, the ground had a slope and they worked their way downward over a bank that led into a gulley. It was more than that though, for the slope kept descending. It was a hollow, and judging from how far they had come already before they reached the bottom it was perhaps an acre in size. It seemed huge in the night, but during the day it would be small. But it offered the best opportunity yet to find a hiding place.

The earth was deeper, and water must have collected in times of rain and persisted during dry spells, for the oaks that grew here were massive and gnarled by age and rot. Many were dead, but their skeletal branches still reached for the sky.

"Quickly," Kareste whispered, and she moved forward.

Faran was not sure what she was doing at first, but she approached one such dead tree, vast in girth. It reached up to the sky with those bare arms of death, and Faran felt a chill.

Then Kareste was gone. She had somehow vanished even as he glanced away momentarily.

"Quickly!" she hissed in a whisper, and he understood.

The vast trunk of the tree was twisted. It was falling, but probably had been for years. The weight of the tree itself, twirling ever so slowly on those hard roots that yet clung deep in the earth had caused a rent in the trunk where rot had weakened it. It was a fissure running from ground level to five feet high, and wide enough that he might slip through it if he turned sideways.

This he did, and it was a tight squeeze, but he was inside the hollowed-out trunk. Kareste was with him, but he could not see her. She had extinguished the faint light even as he had started to move inside, and it was dark as the pit again.

She was not done with magic though. He could not see her, but he felt his skin tingle and sensed her mind. Ever so faintly, his eyes adjusting to the near perfect dark, he saw that she resorted to illusion yet once more. It was as though the trunk of the tree twisted back just a little, and the fissure they had climbed through closed like a door.

"Quiet now," she said almost into his ear. "The woods are alive with elugs."

The proof of that statement came soon after. There was a treading of boots, loud in the dark, and it came to near the tree. Then it passed away. But in moments there was more noise. This time there was a group. Faran was not sure, but he thought there were perhaps a half dozen.

The elugs spoke in their harsh and guttural tongue, and though he did not speak their language he sensed anger and frustration in the words. There was spitting too, another sign of disgust, and stamping of feet in frustration.

An argument broke out, and then they were yelling at each other. Another elug joined them, and his voice was louder than the rest. For a while he yelled at them all, and they sullenly listened. Then they stomped away, continuing the search elsewhere.

Aranloth had told him all about elugs, but he wished he knew what they had said. His training had not extended to their language though, which just now seemed a shortcoming. But it was clear enough that some sort of leader had rebuked them, at length, for failing to find their quarry and then sent them on their way again.

It was near silent for a while again. The din in the woods was far away, and he and Kareste sat down. There was enough room inside the trunk for that, and though it was not comfortable it was better than standing for hours on end.

The dawn was not far away. Faran did not get much sleep. Fear kept him awake at first, and then he took turns with Kareste to maintain the illusion blocking the fissure in the tree.

"Sofanil might detect it," she whispered to him at one point. "But we can hope not. It's very small, and the magic is faint. He might pass by us within a few feet and not know. Hopefully."

So it turned out to be, for they had not been discovered when dawn broke. This they could not really see, but by allowing the illusion to peel back no more than a finger's width on one edge they at times peered out into the outside world.

Such times were brief. Elugs still came and went, and though an hour at a time might pass before they heard any indication of them, yet still they ever returned. They knew their quarry must be close.

They ate a little in the dark interior of the tree. It was a strange feeling, and it was far from comfortable. But they increasingly felt safe here. Though still they knew they could not hide indefinitely. There was always the risk of discovery, and that would more likely be by Sofanil. Nor could they delay their quest to help Aranloth.

Kareste fretted in the dark. At least, for her it was fretting. She muttered at times, even if it was so soft Faran could barely hear. And perhaps, because of the way they had joined minds while spirit walking, he still felt a stronger link to her and intuited more of what she felt than he had ever done before. Maybe to others her mask of lòhren serenity would still be in place, but she could no longer quite hide her feelings from him.

They grew stiff and irritable in the confined space. Both of them knew that come nightfall, they would seek to escape. They had hidden as long as they could and as long as they dared. At any rate, as the afternoon progressed there was no sign at all of elugs.

"Have they moved on?" he whispered.

Her answer came softly to him in the dark. "Many, perhaps. But not all. Some will remain, and now I think they wait silently to set another trap. They know, if we are here, that we might move thinking them gone."

There was a certainty to that view, and Faran agreed with it. The enemy had not given up. They must suspect their quarry had somehow hidden in this wood, and at least some of them would remain, silent and waiting.

It changed nothing though. Surely there were fewer of them than last night. Many must have moved on to scout the grassland, and there would be other woods too.

Night fell, and an owl hooted close by. Faran grinned to himself. Some thought owls an ill omen, but he knew and loved all the creatures of the wild, and just now he loved that owl, for it meant no elug was close.

Kareste knew so as well, for he heard her move. "Time to risk it, Faran."

She led, and very slowly let the illusion drop and moved out of the hollow of the tree. It was dark, yet not as dark as it had been inside. Faran could see the starlit sky in patches above, and the dim outline of trees nearby.

The owl was silent now, or gone elsewhere. Neither he nor Kareste moved, but merely got a sense of the world about them. They stretched their muscles that had become cramped, and let a hundred kinks work their way out of their bodies.

Faran breathed deep of the air, and he was ready for the next stage of their journey. The tombs were close now, and it was better to strike out toward them than hide away inside a tree.

His right hand was ready to reach for the hilt of his sword. In his left hand was his bow. He had command of magic, and he had fought and beaten creatures of the Dark before. He felt strong, but this was a time to rely on stealth. With luck, they could move unobserved through the wood and be far away over the grassland and near the tombs before they were spotted by any elug.

Kareste brushed against him in the dark, and she moved off silently into the trees. She headed north, straight toward their destination.

The hollow they were in was not very large. Soon they tackled a steep slope, the opposite one from where they had come down. It was harder to be quiet here, and they moved with great care.

At length, and without incident, they reached the top. It was a little more open here, and they could see farther. But it was still dim, and everywhere there were deep pools of shadow where an elug could be waiting.

Or they could all be gone. There was no way to know which it was, and the only thing to do was press forward. This they did, and Faran trusted Kareste to see an enemy before them. So he concentrated on listening for any sign they were being followed or any enemy that might come at them from the side.

It was just as well, for they had barely walked more than fifty feet from the hollow when Faran heard an intake of breath from his left. He kicked out instinctively in that direction, and his boot hit something. Then an elug reared up, taken as much by surprise as Faran had been.

There was a moment of hesitation. The elug tried to step back, and in a moment it would yell. But Faran was quicker, and in one movement he drew his sword and hacked. It was not a move that Asana would have been proud of, but it smashed into the helm of the enemy and knocked him down, but it did not stop him from yelling.

A wild cry burst forth, and then was cut off as Faran's sword found the elug's throat on a backhanded swing.

Faran turned to Kareste. One moment her shadowy form was still, and then she ran with him following closely behind.

11. Mercenaries and Magic

Barlan marched ahead of his troops, whistling as he walked.

It was a hard slog through the snow, but this had diminished rapidly as they traveled farther away from Faladir. Why that should be, he was not sure. But he had his suspicions.

All that mattered though was that he was out in the wild. He did not like the city. It hemmed him in. Here, he was free. And in more ways than one.

He had freedom of action, and with that came opportunity. Lindercroft and Savanest had failed. He was now in their place, and if he succeeded in his mission he would reap the benefits. All he had to do was use the magic of the shadow blade on the woman known as Ferla. He could not think of her as the seventh knight. He did not believe in prophecy or destiny or even luck. A man made his own luck by the strength of his will, and he grasped what he wanted and made it his own.

He would not fail here. Too long had he been overlooked. Always it was Lindercroft or Savanest with the king. Of late, Sofanil had his favor.

All that would change though. None of those had his heart. They would balk at things he would not. Power demanded ruthlessness, and there was no one more ruthless than he was.

He whistled louder as he walked, and basked in the faint warmth of the sun. None of them knew just how ruthless he was. But if the chance came, the king would discover it. A knife in the back would kill him as easily as any man. Then the Morleth Stone would be his. Why should that not be? And the kingship after that. Then he could pursue the war against Alithoras that the king was planning. He was going too slow on that, and he was trying too hard to keep his secrets.

But no matter how hard the king tried, they were not hidden. Not from the knights at least. He, like the others, knew of the growing band of elugs. He had not seen them. Few had. But he had his own spies. Little did the king realize that! It was a fault. He trusted in his own strength and the possession of the stone. He thought he was wise. Yet what one man possessed another could steal, and however smart he was another could be smarter still. It was that simple.

The sun grew warmer, and the snow on the track they followed became little more than a dusting. It was, indeed, a pleasant time to be marching despite it being winter.

So it was that in these conditions the troops he had with him marched in good order. They were not soldiers. Barlan was not a fool. He knew regular soldiers would have at least a few spies among them who would report back to the king on all he said and did. No, these were mercenaries, and in some ways they were like him.

A mercenary did what he was told, and he asked no questions. He did not care about the answers, so long as he got paid. At least, these mercenaries were like that. and because he paid them well, he trusted them well. As well as he trusted anyone.

He glanced back at Stonard. He was their captain, and an able soldier too. His mind was quick. He had few scruples, and he kept the men in good order. Some were prone to drinking, which was no great problem. As long as they were fit to march and fit to fight. Stonard told them bluntly they could get drunk if they liked, as long as they did their job.

He had been true to his word, as well. He ignored all their drinking, but had killed a man in front of the others for failing to keep up with the march even as they left the city. That had sobered the rest up, and they would be careful in future.

Stonard saw him glance back and took it as an invitation to start a conversation.

"It's an honor to serve under you, sir. I'll not let you down, and I'll make sure the men don't, either."

Barlan did not doubt that both things were true. Yet the man should have realized that it was a foolish thing to say. Of course they would do their job. If they did not, they would all die, Stonard being the first to do so. Nevertheless, he nodded by way of response and slapped the man on his back.

"I believe you, laddie."

The man grinned. "Perhaps, if time permits, you'll spar with me when we set camp and teach me some of your swordcraft."

"Maybe. Maybe tonight," Barlan answered.

In truth, he did not want to spar this man. It would only embarrass him. He was a good soldier, but he was no match for a knight. But there was a hint of eagerness in his eyes, and Barlan realized why. He thought, just maybe, if he did a good job here he might have an opportunity to become a knight himself. No one had said so to him, but he must have heard rumor that other knights had died on the mission they now undertook themselves, and there were vacancies in the order. It was a foolish, foolish thing to think though. There was far more to being a knight than being good with a sword. He was not up to the task, nor ever would be. Still, he would serve better so long as he thought that was a chance, so there was no reason to disabuse him of his mistaken belief.

"Time for a short break," Barlan said. "We'll be marching fast and hard, but regular rests will enable that."

Stonard went back to the men and gave the order. They wasted no time in sitting down. They knew rests would be short and the days long. They would take full advantage of them, which was proper.

Barlan moved away though. He could talk and joke with soldiers and appear their best friend if he wanted to. But he did not want to just now. He had things to consider.

He dearly wished a report from the elù-drak the king had assigned him, but he would not see her until tonight. She did not like to appear before the men, and they were uncomfortable seeing her also.

That he had been given an elù-drak at all was a sign that the king was unnerved. Recently, he had been keeping them all to himself. "I need them close to hand to keep the city quiet," he had said. There was truth to that statement. And the Shadow Fliers, as the populace liked to call them, were certainly effective at keeping people home at night and instilling fear. But mostly the king just wanted all the power he could gather for himself, and he only grudgingly gave it to others.

He had relented though and given an elù-drak for this mission. Not without argument, but he saw the need for it. Yet still, the one he had given was wounded. Half her face had been burned away. Barlan still found her pretty enough though, in a wild sort of way.

He leaned against a lone pine by the side of the track they followed. He must not think that way. The Shadow Fliers were deadly dangerous. It was in their nature to lure and kill. He knew that, but he was not used to them and it was easy to forget.

Mistakes would kill him. It did not matter if it was with those who served him or the girl he pursued. They were all dangerous in their way, and he reminded himself not to underestimate any of them.

He turned his thoughts to the elù-drak again. She was the best tool he had, and more valuable by far than all the mercenaries put together. They were useless to him unless he found Ferla, but only the elù-drak could do that.

Tonight he would learn if Ferla or her trail had been discovered. There was no point in trying to anticipate that, so he turned his mind instead to Lindercroft and Savanest. They had failed. But why?

It was a puzzle to him. He did not doubt that Ferla was dangerous. So too those who helped her. But to defeat two Morleth Knights was astounding. It was certainly enough reason to be cautious. But he did have an advantage there. He felt the weight of the Shadow Blade in its sheath on his belt. Or maybe he just sensed its cold magic. He was not sure, but he resisted the urge to draw it and look at the blade. He had done that too often, and it was dangerous. But it was also his secret weapon. He did not need to try to kill the girl. Or capture her. He needed only to cut her once, even just a graze, and the prime component of his mission was accomplished. That, surely, was easier than what the others had attempted. He could not fail, nor would he.

The march continued soon after, and though there were many such breaks the mercenaries were haggard by day's end. They were not weak men, but he set the lead and few would be able to follow as easily as he made it look. It was an amusing thought. They did not know he used just a little magic to lend strength to his body, but he did and he enjoyed the thought of them toiling behind him.

Night descended quickly, and there were a few flurries of snow but then that disappeared and the skies cleared to a vast expanse of glittering lights against the dark. He walked away from the camp frequently and looked for the elù-drak, but there was no sign of her. That might be good news, for if she found a trail she would pursue it before she returned.

About midnight he grew restless. The men slept, their campfires burning low to embers. Even Stonard had found his blanket and wrapped himself in it with surly eyes having tried to instigate the sparring session he had wanted without success. He would learn though. Perhaps tomorrow his wish would be granted, but it would be a short session. A knight must show his superiority fast. There could be no sparring with a mere mercenary, but he would draw it out just long enough not to embarrass him completely. That would be counterproductive.

He moved out of sight of the camp, and sat down. It was time to commune with Sofanil and see what he knew. He would rather have learned something from the Night Flier, but as that did not look like happening tonight he would try his luck elsewhere.

The magic came to him quickly these days. He entered the meditative state easily, and let his mind drift on the powers that formed the substance of the universe. Magic some called it. Science Aranloth had termed it on a time, but names did not really matter. All that mattered was that he had use of the skill.

He found Sofanil swiftly. It was not hard. All the knights were linked to the king, and to each other, as well as the Morleth Stone. They were separate, but in some senses one. The sorcery of the stone ran through them all, and he knew he could find any of them no matter where they were over the vastness of Alithoras.

Sofanil sensed him even before he formed an image of himself in the smoke of a campfire many leagues away that bent to a breeze not blowing where Barlan himself sat.

"Hail, Knight Barlan," came the voice in his mind. "The king informs me that you have been sent to search for the girl. What news?"

That was just like Sofanil. He thought to take charge by asking questions first.

Barlan felt his temper bubble to the surface, but he suppressed it. The more his enemies upset him, the friendlier he was.

"Hail, Knight Sofanil. I have nothing to report. But it's good to commune with someone who understands our great task. I'm only just now heading out from Faladir, but is there anything I can do to assist you?"

Sofanil considered that as though it were his due, and Barlan felt the urge to grind his teeth but he smiled instead. He had no fear that his offer could be taken up though. There was little he could do to help the other man, and if something were asked he would find a way to claim it interfered with his mission direct from the king.

"No. I have things under control and exactly as I wish them. Faran and the lòhren Kareste will shortly be caught in one or another of my traps."

That was good news. Sofanil would get credit for it, but Ferla was now the prize, and Barlan was sure he would find her first.

"You can tell me this though," Sofanil continued. "I have been unable to commune with Savanest. Has the king said anything to you about him?"

Barlan pretended to look thoughtful. "No. He's said nothing to me."

Once, he had found it hard to lie. But that seemed a long time ago now. Lies fell from his lips like sunlight from the sky, and he found joy in the deception. Yet he did sense that Sofanil was uneasy. Perhaps he was not believed, but it would be unnerving to try to commune with another knight and fail. Perhaps it was just that.

"Very well," came the reply. "Keep in touch."

That was all Sofanil said, and then he broke the communion swiftly. Barlan did grind his teeth at that tone now that he could not be seen, and his mood was dark. But it improved as he looked up and saw the elù-drak circling in to land. Hopefully, she brought good news with her.

12. Trapped

Kareste fleeted through the woods like a ghost. Faran was her silent shadow.

The dead elug lay behind them, and safety ahead if they could reach it. Faran could not tell if there was a pursuit. Had they been seen or heard?

All around the woods seemed dark and menacing. But he neither heard nor saw any other sign of life. Yet while running, his senses were dimmed and he could not be sure.

Kareste came to a swift halt. They stood now on the edge of the wood. Before them opened up the grassland again, little more than a dark ocean in the night. Anything could be out there, and they might not see it. They would still have to venture into it though.

He listened intently, turning half back the way they had come. The wood was silent, and it seemed that few elugs were left within it and the one he had killed had not been heard.

Turning to the front, Kareste was gazing at him, her eyes near invisible but he could still tell she fixed him with all her attention. She had been looking to the front and would trust his assessment of any danger behind.

He shook his head, but did not even dare whisper. Her figure seemed to relax though, and instead of rushing out into the night she walked at a careful pace.

They moved with great care. By some stroke of fortune they had not been detected, and Kareste fully intended to take advantage of that. They did not rest as they walked through the night. She was putting as much distance as possible between them and the wood, and if she did not travel swiftly then at least it was ceaseless.

No breeze blew. The night was still. There were no animals nor even the cry of a distant owl. Once, they heard a scurrying sound in the dark. Faran did not think it was an elug. More likely a badger that had been startled. But it was disturbing that there had been only the one indication of some other creature out here with them. It was as though nature had gone to ground, wary of some hunter that roamed the shadows.

Faran knew who that hunter was. Elugs. They had seen none, nor been seen themselves. Yet he knew with increasing certainty that they were out here, spread out. Were they sleeping? Were they still searching? He did not know, but he knew they were there and come daylight he wanted to be as close as possible to the tombs. He feared going in there, but he feared staying out here as well.

The eastward horizon lightened, and the starry sky faded. In the distance, the dawn chorus of birds sang of life with all their hearts, but it was silent near Faran and Kareste as they hastened cautiously like foxes heading back to their den after the night's foraging.

Even as the sun rose and streaked golden light over the green grass, cries rang out from the east.

"Elugs!" cursed Kareste, and she broke into a smooth run. It was not a sprint. They were too far from safety for that.

Faran located the enemy. They were a quarter of a mile away, and as they ran toward their quarry long shadows from the rising sun loped ahead of them.

The chase had begun as Faran had feared all night that it must. But despite his armor he ran smoothly, his long strides covering the ground with an easy speed that he could keep up for hours. And even as he was burdened by armor, so too were those who pursued.

Kareste did not seem overly disturbed. She ran smoothly, and he knew she was slowing her pace for him. He wondered what other tricks she had, for illusion could not work now. Not when it would be expected and the quarry was already in plain sight.

"It's not far to the tombs now," she said breathlessly as she ran. "Courage!"

She had no sooner said that than there were more cries lifting up into the sky from the east. A separate group of elugs clambered up over the rim of one of the many gulleys in the area.

"Sofanil!" Kareste hissed.

Faran had seen the elugs, but he had not seen the knight. He did now though, and he felt the first twinges of panic creeping through him. The urge came upon him to run faster but he resisted that. This was a race, and he must pace himself well or he would die. Panic had no part to play in survival.

The first group of elugs had fallen in almost behind them now, but the new group seemed less inclined to veer toward them and close the gap than they did to run parallel on the eastern side.

"He seeks to cut us off from the tombs," Kareste said breathily as she ran. "He knows where we go."

They were close to a river now, and a line of trees showed its progress through the grassland. In the east, beyond Sofanil and the elugs, Faran could see sunlight shine off the strange building that once, even if it seemed a very long time ago now, they had emerged from the tombs with Aranloth.

"He *has* cut us off," Faran replied. He was glad that no panic had crept into his voice. He had the training and the skills of a knight. He would face death, if he must, calmly.

Kareste glanced at him. Her face was strained, and her breath came in deep gulps, but she still spoke to him.

"It is not the end yet, Faran. Have I not said that there are many ways into the tombs? Some in plain sight, and others hidden."

She said no more, but her words gave him hope as she had intended.

They ran onward. At one point they came to the crest of a slight rise. Here, Kareste paused to look ahead and determine her route. Faran hoped she knew exactly where she was going. He took the opportunity to string his bow and wing an arrow toward the elugs approaching from the rear. It was a long shot, but he struck one hapless elug in the thigh. They paused, worried now, and those among them who had their own bows sent a volley of arrows in return.

Faran watched them fall well short. Their short bows were no match for his Dromdruin hunter's bow.

"Quickly," Kareste called, and the race began again.

Faran did not loose any more arrows. He would keep them in reserve until the enemy was close enough that he could be sure of a killing shot. Each of them he eliminated this way would be one less to fight hand to hand later.

The ground sloped downward. The long line of trees came close. Even above the wind in his ears and the pounding of blood in his body, he thought he could hear the distant roar of the great waterfall where the river spilled over the escarpment in a great rush.

Suddenly they were running down a steep slope. The grass had changed to a track of hard-packed sand, and a steep embankment rose to the left. In that sandy soil he saw many small holes dug out by kingfishers for nests, and then they were past that and down to a flat shore of loose rocks and sand.

The river ran before them, from left to right. The water was almost still close to the shore, but far out in the middle he saw a swift current.

The enemy was closing in fast behind them. To the left and right was a long expanse of empty shore. But quite a distance down the right-hand shore Sofanil and his group of elugs poured down a similar bank to the one Faran had just descended. They swung toward their quarry when they reached the bottom, screaming and waving swords in triumph.

Kareste had got it wrong. There was no entrance to the tombs here, hidden or otherwise. They were trapped.

13. Dangerous Plans

Menendil ate the last of his slice of seed cake. It was one of his favorites, and Norla made the best he had ever eaten. But he had not enjoyed it as much today as usual.

He, Norgril and Caludreth were seated around the small table in Caludreth's room. It was still early in the morning, at least early enough that no customers had arrived yet. That would change shortly though. Since the cold spell had broken, there had been a small but steady stream of folks seeking drink, companionship and food.

The merchant and his servants had left, but his arrival had signaled a change in the city. The people had cowered until then, locked up by both the extraordinary cold spell and fear. But no strong and free people put up with that forever. Cautiously, but with determination, they took up their lives again.

For some, that meant coming to the Bouncing Stone Inn, and Menendil was glad of it.

He glanced at Caludreth, finishing his own slice of seed cake. He had not told the once-knight what he intended, but they had started to discuss that it was time the Hundred acted again.

"We toppled the statue," Menendil said. "But that was a while ago. No doubt, other such statues around the city are being watched now. There may be traps set for us. So we must avoid repeating our actions and instead look to do something new."

Caludreth absently brushed a few crumbs from his lips and eyed him shrewdly.

"You have something in mind, yes?"

Norgril barked out a sharp laugh. "Does he ever!"

The once-knight raised an eyebrow at that. "Then by all means, tell me your plan."

"You may not like it," Menendil replied.

"That may be. Or it may not. But either way, you are the leader of the Hundred. I will of course give my advice and my help, but the power of decision is yours. You lead, and the Hundred follows. And myself as well."

Menendil had been surprised for some while at Caludreth's attitude to this. He had been a Kingshield Knight, and he was the best warrior and the wisest mind among them, yet he still deferred to a simple publican, even if that publican had once been in the army.

It was a sign of confidence in him, as well as courtesy. Yet there were times when Menendil would have been more than happy to pass on the weight of leadership to another.

He cleared his throat. "You know a merchant stayed overnight and left this morning with all his men?"

"I do indeed. They made enough racket as they left."

Menendil smiled at that. It was always the case that those leaving early made a lot of noise thinking they were in fact being quiet. But those same folks would be the first to complain if someone else did it to them. It was human nature, and he was glad that Caludreth probably shared the same foibles as normal people. Otherwise, he would have seemed unapproachable.

"Well," Menendil went on, "he was a grain merchant, and he gave me some interesting news."

Caludreth looked at him closely. He could not have guessed Menendil's plan so quickly, but it was unnerving the way the man seemed to know what others were thinking.

"He sold his grain to the king. At least, to agents of the king. He was of the belief the king is building an army. I mean a new army, over and above the regular one."

"It's not unexpected."

"You think the rumor is true, then?"

"Of course," Caludreth replied. "I learned the nature of the Morleth Stone as part of my training as a knight. Legends told throughout the city might be more colorful, but at heart they're all quite correct. The stone is ultimate evil, and the king has been subverted by it. Its nature, and that now means the king's nature, is to turn everything into its own likeness. Neither king nor stone will be satisfied with Faladir. Both will seek to conquer all lands and change them by fire and sword into what they are themselves. The Shadow cannot tolerate freedom or individuality. In that way it is the opposite of the Light, which celebrates personal choice and differences."

Menendil had never heard it put like that before, and it disturbed him how Caludreth spoke of the stone as if it were alive. But what he had said made sense.

"Then this is what I think the Hundred must do next. We have to keep hope alive that the seventh knight is coming. We've done well so far, but we have to continue striking. The grain enables us a double opportunity. If we destroy it, we can encourage hope and show that not even deadly cold and the terror of elù-draks daunt us. And at the same time we can deprive the king's army of what it needs to march on other lands."

Caludreth turned to Norgril. "What do you think?"

"I like it. We must be bold. What we don't do now, we may never be able to do in the future because the king's power is growing. Yet I do have one concern, and I know Mender shares it."

"What concern is that?" Caludreth asked.

"A fearful one," Norgril replied. "If grain is in short supply, the king might direct it to the army and let the city starve."

It was not a good prospect, but quite a possible one and none of them liked it.

"Would burning the warehouses even destroy the grain?" Caludreth asked.

Menendil had considered that. "So far as I've been able to reason, only the surface would burn. Especially if it's kept in bags. But there may be silos there as well. A lot would depend on how hot the fire got, but I'm thinking smoke would do most of the damage. The grain would reek of it and be inedible. Not to mention that just as much, or more, would be destroyed by water as men attempted to put the fire out."

There was quiet for a while as they all thought on that.

"Perhaps we can steal it instead?" ventured Norgril.

"That would have an advantage," Caludreth replied. "If we possessed the grain, we could ensure it reached the citizens of Faladir. But the warehouses must contain many, many tons. How could we steal it? It would take days of working in plain sight."

No one had an answer to that. Menendil had contemplated the idea earlier himself, but he had not fathomed a way to do it without being caught.

"What about this, instead?" he said at length as inspiration struck him. "We burn down some warehouses, but we pick the ones close to the grain rather than the ones with the grain itself. If the king is gathering food for an army, then there would be other equipment nearby."

Caludreth brought his hand down on the table with a slap and a laugh.

"That will do!" he said. "Yes, that will do nicely. It shows the king is still being resisted, and at the same time it damages his capacity to prosecute a war. Well done, Mender."

Norgril placed a hand on his shoulder. "I agree. Very nicely worked out."

Menendil was not so sure himself. It solved some of their problems, but it would still be very dangerous.

"The king is unlikely to leave either grain or equipment unguarded though. That might give us some big problems."

Caludreth nodded. "They will certainly be guarded. We have to expect that. So, this will have to be a mission of stealth. Just a few people must go, for they will have the best chance of eluding the watchers and escaping undetected. A larger group would instill suspicion instantly."

They looked at each other for a few moments in silence then. Their words had taken on the weight of a decision made. But there was an unspoken decision too. Having made the choice, and restricting the mission to just a few, they all knew it would be them who would undertake it. There was no need to endanger others. At least, not for this mission.

"Just us three, then?" Caludreth said casually.

"Aye," Menendil replied.

"Count me in," Norgril said almost at the same time.

Menendil took down their plates to the kitchen after that. Absently, he washed them while his wife worked at the table getting food ready for the lunchtime trade.

He glanced at her, but he did not have the heart to say what was on his mind. How could he tell her that he was risking his life again? Or worse, that if he were captured he was risking hers?

He steeled himself to do it though. It would not be acceptable to just leave tonight, for tonight they would surely put their plan into action, and leave her wondering what they were doing.

He walked over to the table, pulled a chair out and sat down.

14. Do You Trust Me?

Faran calmly notched an arrow. He trusted his skill with a bow, and he knew he would make the enemy pay dearly for every step they took in his direction.

"Put that away," commanded Kareste. "And follow me."

Faran was surprised, for he could see no alternative to what he was doing, but he complied quickly. Kareste was a lòhren, and when she took that tone he had learned to obey.

She waded out into the river. Again, he was surprised, for with armor and sword he would not be able to swim. Especially if they went out into the stronger current. But again, he followed.

Sofanil was approaching from the side, but the elugs who had been behind came screaming down the embankment toward them. They shouted and hooted, for the chase had come to an end. They knew it would not be possible to swim the river, and their enemy was trapped. They could be picked off by arrows where they stood in the water, or if they came back to the shore they could be hacked down by swords.

Kareste gripped his arm. "Do you trust me, Faran?"

"Of course."

"Then what we do now will be difficult, but it can be done. Your armor will make it hard, but I'll help you and the distance won't be long."

"Help me to do what?"

"There's no time. Just do what I do, and trust me."

She paused briefly and looked back up the bank. For a moment, he thought she was watching the elugs race toward them, but then he realized she was ignoring them entirely. Instead, she seemed to be lining herself up with some landmark she saw there, for she moved a few paces to the side and then nodded to herself in some kind of affirmation.

"Take a deep breath, hold it and swim," she commanded again. "I'll help you, and it'll be over in a moment."

He did as asked, and before he knew it she had pulled him down by the arm and under the water which was nearly to their waists.

Panic rose up in him, but he fought it down. The rush of the water was in his ears, and he could barely see. But Kareste's hand was still on his arm, and she pulled him forward.

The weight of the armor dragged him down. The strung bow looped over his shoulder was awkward. But Kareste's strength was great, and she pulled him onward and he kicked back as best he could to propel himself.

He caught a blurred glimpse of some sort of arched doorway. It seemed to him that they were going down now rather than forward, but he was disorientated and confused.

If not for Kareste, he knew he would have died. Even with her there, guiding him and pulling him on through the dark, he was not sure he was going to survive. He felt the urge to breathe, but could not. He felt his limbs grow tired, and if they failed him he was dead, too. There was no turning back.

Kareste's voice sounded in his mind, calm and assured above the rush of water in his ears.

Nearly there, Faran. Swim.

He swam on, but now he knew he was mostly being pulled forward by her, and he marveled at her strength. Yet even as his lungs burned and fatigue turned his body to lead, his feet scraped a hard surface. Several more times they did so, and he knew it was no riverbed but smooth stone.

On the verge of passing out, suddenly there was light. His feet caught hold of the floor, and then his knees and arms. He crawled forward now, Kareste hauling him onward, and suddenly his head rose above water and he saw they were in a chamber of some kind.

He paid no heed to it. Crawling onward until he was out of the water he heaved for breath, and nothing seemed sweeter in his life than the simple act of breathing.

Kareste let him go while he recovered. As he lay panting on the floor she stood and faced back the way they had come. He had forgotten they had enemies after them, and he tried to struggle to his feet.

"Be still and rest, Faran," Kareste instructed him. "They'll not follow us in here. Elugs fear water and don't swim."

That was reassuring. Yet still she watched the opening, her staff in hand and a steady light coming from its tip, and he knew she could not be certain. Sofanil might drive them to it, or he might come himself.

Slowly, he stood. Water dripped off him, and he shivered. Despite what they had just done, his quiver was still on his back and he still had his bow. Most of all, he still had his sword. That had been more likely to drag him down and kill him than be lost, but now that they were through it reassured him just by its presence.

"What of Sofanil?" he asked, his breathing still raspy. "Do you think he will follow?"

"Not by himself, I think. But even if he does, we're in the tombs now. Or nearly. I believe we only have to go into the next chamber to be at risk of the harakgar, but I'm not sure of that. Keep your eyes open. If he comes, we will go there and he cannot follow."

They rested a while, and watched the pool of water out of which they themselves had come. It did not stir, and as Faran got his breath back he glanced around the chamber. It was nothing special, being made of some type of brick, if neatly fitted together. Age had not marred it greatly, though the flagstone floor showed signs of inundation by water and drying out.

The chamber was spherical, and empty of any decoration. The vaulted ceiling above was not high, and he surmised that they were somewhere under the bank with the kingfisher nests that they had raced down before. It was a strange feeling, knowing what lay above and that it was close, and yet also exceedingly dangerous to reach and hidden to all the world. Perhaps only Aranloth and Kareste knew of this place, and now him.

At the far side of the chamber was an archway, the strange writing of the Letharn who built this place carved into the stone. He did not want to know what it said. He guessed it was a warning not to enter the tombs, and one he would like to heed, if he could. That was not an option though, and he stopped himself from thinking that way. A task that was dreaded became even harder than it was in reality.

The light in the chamber moved, and Faran's shadow rose up against the far wall as Kareste turned toward him.

"Are you rested enough to walk?" she asked.

"I am. I'll just get ready, though."

He unstrung his bow. The string, thoroughly wet, would greatly impair performance. So too the wet and heavier arrows. These he took out of the quiver and ensured there was no water trapped in it. The fletching would be damaged now too, but not enough to stop him from using them in the future.

When he was ready he nodded, and Kareste took one last glance back at the pool.

"This was a place of testing," she said. "The Letharn knew the water level would rise and fall, but they planned for the entrance to be underwater at all times. Initiates of the wizard-priests were meant to enter as we have, and it was part of their testing."

Faran grimaced. It would have been hard for them, but they had not worn armor. At least he did not think so. It was strange to think that all that time ago, and a vast amount of years it was too, Aranloth himself had once come through that terrifying tunnel of water and up into this very chamber.

"Let's go," Kareste said, then she paused and looked at him. "Do you remember the charm?"

"I remember." It was something he would never forget. That charm was the difference between life and death in this place, and it was graven into his memory forever.

They passed through the arched entrance and into the tombs themselves. Here was the domain of the harakgar, and if there were a greater magic in all Alithoras, Faran had not heard of it in his studies.

The harakgar were the highest triumph of the magic of the greatest empire ever to have risen in the land. Or, as some held, and Faran was not sure they were wrong, the gravest sin of a people whose power outgrew their wisdom.

It was dark, and the light from Kareste's staff did not seem to brighten the passageway as it should. The dark pressed back against it. At least, so it seemed, but Faran had been here before and knew that fear lent strength to imaginings. He must be on his guard, both against the harakgar and also his own mental weakness.

The passageway was narrow. They were in the tombs, but no burials had ever taken place here. This had been a place of testing for initiates Kareste had told him. He could not help but wonder what trials they faced. At least he had Kareste with him, and she knew what she was doing. But he felt pity for those who had long ago come this way and for a different purpose. Their lives had been harder than his, and he guessed that some of those who began their testing here did not live to come to its end.

Beneath them, the floor dried out quickly. There was no sign that water had ever come this far, and he realized that they had been walking at a slight angle upwards since coming out of the water. There was nothing here, save the smooth floor and walls that felt tight and constraining, as though they might fall and crush anything inside at any moment. That too was his imagination.

Faran tried to think of other things. His mind latched on to the harakgar, for they were a pressing danger. Yet he knew it was not wise to focus too much on them. Fear would grow the more he did so, and besides, they had not shown themselves yet. Better to think of Sofanil. He at least was an enemy they had left behind. Although he could not quite be sure of that.

"None of the knights know the charm to enter this place?" he asked. "There is no way they could have discovered it?"

"No. There is no way. Few know the charm, very few indeed. Only those that Aranloth has told in person. It's not recorded anywhere, nor can it be discovered by magic."

That was what he wanted to hear. He had known it himself anyway, but just now he wanted some reassurance.

Kareste kept on speaking though, and what she said next was less reassuring.

"Nevertheless, I won't underestimate Sofanil. He's the smartest of the knights, and though he cannot enter here, he still worries me."

15. Corridor of Fear

They moved forward along the narrow tunnel, and Faran strained his eyes in the dim light. Yet he saw nothing of the harakgar.

Kareste must have guessed what he was thinking, but that was probably not difficult.

"They don't always appear straight away, but they know we are here. The moment any living thing enters the tombs, they know."

Faran did not doubt it. "But why do they delay coming, then? They have never done that before."

Kareste laughed softly in the dark. "Be wary of assumptions. You say they have never done that before, but you have only been here *once* before. The harakgar know you now, and they know you are back. Their tactics may change. I, who have been here several times, have seen that. Likely they'll do something different. Or maybe not. Never think that you know what will happen because the moment you do you become ripe for falling into a trap. That applies not just to the harakgar."

What she said was true, and he realized his mistake. He had thought he knew something, when in fact he did not. His expectations had outrun his logic, and it was an error. It amused him though to think that he would always be learning. No matter his training or his experience, there was always something else to know, or an attitude to be wary of. Strangely, he found that comforting. Knowledge had no bounds, and that encouraged him to keep learning. The mind that was only half full was easier to fill than the one already brimming over.

The tunnel took a sharp turn to the left. It remained narrow and unadorned, but it began to descend, and after a short while it did so steeply. They were moving deep into the earth now.

Soon they came to a winding circle of stairs. These turned halfway around and opened up into a kind of landing before plunging downward again. Faran studied the small chamber, and it was different from the tunnel. Here, although there were no images as often decorated the walls of the tombs, there was writing and a small stone bench. Likely, it was a place to sit and rest.

"There are several such places as these," Kareste said. "Nine in total, if I remember rightly. Here the initiate would answer a question posed by a wizard-priest. If they could not answer correctly, they had a choice of going on or going back. But to go on meant they must get the remainder of the questions right, or be killed."

More and more Faran had respect for those initiates of long ago. Theirs was a tough life, and he began to wonder about the Letharn. Certainly they had raised the greatest empire ever to rule in Alithoras, but were they good?

It was not his place to judge. How could he, looking back from where the world now stood, decide on the morals of another age with different problems? This much he knew, though. The Letharn were always under threat. There were other empires, and they all sought dominion. That meant subduing their opposition. The wizard-priests had held not only great power but a massive burden of responsibility. It was their magic that fought the sorcery of their enemies. If they were weak, they would be defeated and the people they were charged with protecting would be enslaved.

This much he knew from history, though. It was always thus. When the leaders of a society became weak and corrupt, the society would fall. No matter that it was a village or the greatest nation on earth. If enemies did not overrun them, they would fall from within by treachery.

Kareste led him down the stairs, and each of these little chambers with a bench and writing on the wall was the same. Except, he thought, for the writing. That seemed different each time.

They passed through the last one, and then the tunnel ran straight and true again, neither sloping up nor down. If his bearings were correct, it seemed that they now moved under the river. It was strange to think of all the weight of rock above, and stranger still to think of the water above that. But this was the Tombs of the Letharn, and all things were possible and the stranger something was the more likely it was to be true.

The tunnel was not the same as before though. To each side were irregularly spaced alcoves. At first, he thought they would be burials, for this was how the ancients had used those parts of the tombs that he had been in before. But the alcoves were empty, and there was no sign that any interments had ever occurred.

Kareste saw him looking curiously into each as they walked past.

"Wizard-priests hid in these alcoves," she told him. "As the initiates went by, they attacked them. Mostly with magic, but sometimes by weapons as well. If they fought well enough, they were allowed to move on."

This seemed crueler and crueler to Faran, but it was a rite of passage that only the strongest could survive. Yet cruel or not, it produced the likes of Aranloth, so it could not be all bad.

He soon discovered though that this passageway of testing was no mere harsh trial. Death was a very real possibility. As they walked, they began to see ancient bodies on the floor. The clothing had often rotted with the withered flesh, and here and there parts of skulls where the leathery skin had drawn away gleamed in Kareste's dim light.

"They left the dead initiates here to serve as a warning to new ones," Kareste informed him.

It was a warning, and Faran took it. In this place death lay in wait for the unwary. If he were not careful he would lie in this place too, dead, and his dreams turned to dust.

"The Letharn could be harsh," Kareste went on to say. "They expected much of the wizard-priests, and only the strongest survived. Only the strongest could protect the nation from its enemies."

They moved ahead, but they did so cautiously. Kareste tilted her staff and began to study the floor with the dim light. She went a little way like this, and in one place where there were more bodies than usual she let out a sudden hiss.

"There it is," she said, pointing directly at the floor with her staff.

All Faran saw was a line across the floor about two feet wide and running from one wall to the other. The stone was just slightly a different shade, though that was hard to tell for the layer of dust that lay over it.

"What is it?"

"A trap. Pressure triggered it, and spears were hurtled from the wall."

Faran looked at the wall. He saw nothing, then he looked higher and spotted a series of small holes. Looking to the opposite wall, he saw the same thing.

It would have been an effective trap. All the more so for the bodies on the floor would have drawn the eye and there would be less chance of seeing the holes and deducing their purpose.

"It would be dismantled now, I suppose?" he asked.

Kareste shook her head. "No. The ancients did not rely entirely on the harakgar for the defense of this place. Nor does Aranloth, the last of them left alive. Probably the mechanisms no longer work, but that's not something we're going to put to the test."

She leaped nimbly across the faint line on the floor, and Faran did likewise. He did not look back as they continued.

There was still no sign of the harakgar, and Faran found that increasingly disconcerting. He did not want to see them again, but the thought kept entering his mind that they were watching and biding their time. They would strike when his and Kareste's attention lapsed. That was what he feared, and he knew that by their failure to appear they might well be deliberately trying to lull their opponents. Almost, he would prefer it if they showed themselves. That way their danger would be front of mind.

The corridor of fear went on for a while, but soon the alcoves ceased to line the sides. The walls widened out slightly too, and the sense of restrained space and the weight of the world above reduced.

They came to an archway, and this was of some white stone. Faran thought it was quartz, but his tuition in the types of stones of the earth had been limited. It was beautiful though, and contrasted sharply with the passageway they had just walked.

Kareste turned to him, and her expression, though calm, was serious.

"This is a place to be wary of," she warned him. "There is magic here older even than the harakgar. All is illusion, but it will not seem so. I would rather not have come this way, but Sofanil forced us. Be careful. Stay wary. Trust in your rational mind, for this is a place of testing just as much as the passage we have passed through. It is a place where your greatest fears can seem real."

She moved through the archway, and Faran walked confidently after her. She may not have wanted to come this way, but she would not have brought him if the danger was too great. What he saw when he passed the threshold surprised him though. It was a great circular chamber, lined and domed with quartz, and the light dazzled him. It was not from Kareste's staff, but rather a wall of light itself, like a curtain, drawn across the middle of the room and rising to the highest parts of the dome.

16. Holding Back Truths

Kareste looked into the wall of light. Nothing could be seen through it, but she knew what was beyond and what was about to happen.

She turned to Faran. Never before had she wanted to help him so much, but what was about to begin could not be prepared for. No amount of training would help. It was better to go in on short notice. More than that, she believed in him, and that he would get through this, but guilt washed over her too. What if she was wrong?

"Remember," she said again. "All is illusion. This is magic and not reality."

That was all she had time to say. Even as she spoke the wall of light drew forward. Swift it came, and there was no chance to step back. It rolled over her, and the brightness increased until it hurt her eyes and she could see nothing.

There was a sensation of movement though, as if the light had picked her up and by the power of the magic that formed it carried her elsewhere.

The light faded, and she stumbled to the ground. Quickly she rose, not sure what to expect except that she would be tested by her greatest fear. She looked around and saw that she was in a chamber, and she knew it. She knew it well, for it was the Great Hall in Lòrenta, the fortress of the lòhrens and their home when not wandering the land. *Her* home.

Almost immediately she began to forget that she was not really here. It was illusion. She stood inside the wall of light in the Tombs of the Letharn, but that truth began to fade from her mind and what she saw now became her reality.

The Council of Lòhrens was assembled, the Lòhrenin as it was called. It was the ruling body of twelve that governed all that the lòhrens did and stood for. Only there were eleven there now. The twelfth, and their head, was not present.

"Aranloth cannot speak for you now," one of the hooded figures proclaimed. "He is dead."

Kareste steadied herself. Aranloth had always been her advocate even when others opposed her. She need not fear this man, or the others.

But she did. They held authority, and she had failed them and all the lòhrens in the past. With Aranloth dead, they would expel her from the order.

No! This was illusion. The thought danced briefly across her mind. This was illusion, and Aranloth was not dead. Not yet anyway.

Another of the council stepped a pace forward and looked down on her.

"You have never been a true lòhren. Aranloth, wise though he was, erred about you. You let us down before. You have done so again."

Kareste felt her temper rising. "I have atoned for my failures. I still atone for them. The seventh knight lives because of me, and she is ready for the task set for her. I have risked all for her, and for Faran. They will fulfil their destinies, and I have played my role as a lòhren to ensure they have that chance."

A third member of the council stepped forward. He pulled back his hood and showed his face. He was a younger man, and his eyes were dark and a trimmed black beard grew where she had expected a longer silvery one. Who he was, she did not know. But it was clear that the leadership of the lòhrens was changing.

"Fool girl," he said. His voice was soft but filled with confidence. He knew of what he spoke, and she did not doubt it.

"The seventh knight is hunted again. She will not live to see Faladir. But had you stayed with her, she might have had the chance to fulfil her destiny. You erred in leaving her, and now the Morleth Stone will spread its darkness across all Alithoras."

Kareste remained calm. "I had no choice. Aranloth needs me, and Ferla has the best of companions in Asana and Kubodin. They'll not let her down."

"They are yet others that you have failed. Are these warriors, Asana and Kubodin, lòhrens with the skill to oppose dark sorcery? They too will die because of your folly."

To that, she had no answer. It was what she had feared herself.

The first lòhren spoke again. "You let your friendship with Aranloth sway you from the path of duty to protect the seventh knight. You failed, and all for nothing because Aranloth is dead and beyond your reach."

"Aranloth is not dead. Not yet. I go to rescue him, if I can."

"No. You do not. You stand before us to plead your case why you should not be stripped of your lòhren's staff. Your quest is over, and our judgement of you will soon be given."

Kareste felt as though the room spun on her, but she focused on the closest lòhren and addressed him.

"I have given my life to the cause of the lòhrens, and if I have failed it has not been through lack of effort. If Aranloth were here, he would rebuke you."

The first lòhren gripped his staff more tightly, and he spoke in a stern voice.

112

"Aranloth is not here, and the right of rebuke is ours." The lòhrens gathered behind him and murmured their agreement.

Kareste was about to speak again when a fourth lòhren stepped forward.

"You invoke Aranloth's name, as well you might. He was your friend, and he always spoke on your behalf. It was by the strength of his will alone, despite our objections, that you were raised to our high order. After you had been cast out, it was he alone that supported your return. And having returned you have failed yet again. Nor do I just mean the seventh knight."

"I do not concede that I have failed the seventh knight. All our destinies stand upon the edge of a knife, and it is true that she may fail. Likely even, given the forces arrayed against her. But those are the chances of the world, and even a lòhren cannot guard against all ill fortune."

Yet another lòhren stepped forward, and Kareste felt that she was overmatched. How could she defend herself against them all? But she stood taller, and she resolved that no matter what they said she would not succumb to self-doubt.

"We have already judged you for your failure to succor the seventh knight. We speak now of your next failure, and in its way perhaps the worst. For in this matter you not only failed but lied, and that is a sin greater than folly."

Despite her resolve, Kareste felt the shadow of doubt creep over her. She knew what this charge would be.

The lòhren continued. "You have lied to the young man Faran. He would not have agreed to this fool's errand to save Aranloth had you not deceived him."

Those words cut like a knife, and Kareste took a step back.

"In truth," she admitted, "guilt lies heavily upon me. But I don't think you are right. Faran would have come with me even if he knew what I knew. Nor have I deceived him, though it is certainly true that I have hidden things from him."

The lòhren shook his head slowly. "If you believed he would have come, then why did you not tell him?"

That was the crux of the matter. "I did not tell him because the telling would not change his actions, but it would weigh him down with fear. Why place that burden on him until he had to bear it?"

"Because it is the truth!"

"The truth can be a dangerous thing. It can do more damage than a lie."

"It is not for you to decide." Again, there was a soft murmur of agreement from the council of lòhrens.

"And yet—"

Kareste got no further with what she was going to say. The lòhrens shuffled toward her, and they were all hooded again and menacing.

"Judgement is passed," they declaimed in one voice, resonant with power.

They came closer. "You are stripped of your staff."

The lòhrens gathered close, authority booming in their voices. "You are cast from our order."

Again, they drew closer, and now they towered above her.

"You are condemned to death."

The lòhrens raised their staffs high and pointed the tips toward her. She could not fight them. They were too many and too strong. Here, she would die.

But a voice whispered in her mind, and it was her own. Was this real, or illusion?

Kareste gathered herself, and she leaned upon her staff in a posture of calmness.

"You have no authority over me. You are my fear only, and while I acknowledge you, yet still I believe in my choices. They were right."

Even as she spoke, the towering lòhrens leapt up like tongues of flame, and they turned and twisted into a wall of light that flung her down.

With a boom like a clap of thunder, she was thrown to the ground. But she knew where she was again. Around her was the spherical chamber in the Tombs of the Letharn. The wall of light was behind her now. She had come through it, but she spun around looking for Faran.

He was nowhere to be seen.

17. The Truth

Faran watched the wall of light, and even as he did it rolled toward him swifter than he could react. It burst over him like a thousand suns, and blinded and dizzy he fell to the floor.

He rolled and stood up again, drawing his sword, but the world seemed to spin and roil as though it was moving. Bracing himself, he swayed to and fro.

Gradually, his vision returned and the light faded to normal day. He looked around, disbelieving where he was.

This was a place that he knew, and could never forget. He knew every house that faced him, every porch, every garden and every cottage. He knew the beaten track upon which he stood. The forest all around was as familiar as his own thoughts, and the glimpses he saw of high ridges were places that he knew and loved.

He stood in the center of the village of Dromdruin, and by some great miracle it was restored. Lindercroft had burned and murdered here, yet that history was gone. Or perhaps it had never happened. Was this some new reality, and a better one?

The sword felt heavy in his hand, but before he could sheathe it a figure came into view. He could not see it clearly, for twilight began to creep through the surrounding forest and long shadows lay over the road.

This much was clear though. The man who approached was a Kingshield Knight, and he walked with grace and assurance. The sword that was in his hand seemed familiar, like everything else, and there was something disturbingly familiar about the figure too.

The knight drew close, and a hollow voice sounded from within the helm.

"Hail, Knight Faran, and welcome to Dromdruin."

There was something very wrong about all this, but Faran was not even sure what it was. How had he come to be here? But he *was* here, and Dromdruin was somehow whole again.

"I am not a knight," he replied.

The other man laughed. "You deny who you are just as you deny what you have done."

"I'm Faran, but I'm not a knight."

The other man looked him up and down. "Do you not wear the armor of a Kingshield Knight?"

"I do, but—"

"And is not that sword at your side a knight's sword?"

"Yes, however—"

"And are you not trained in the ways of the knights? You possess skill with that blade, do you not? And magic. So too have you benefited from the learning of history and philosophy and all the other arts of a knight."

Faran took a slow breath. "All of that is true, but I'm *not* a Kingshield Knight."

The other man seemed amused. "You deceive yourself, Faran. If you see a tree with roots in the ground and a trunk with branches covered in leaves and reaching for the sun, would you not call it a tree?"

Faran had no answer to that. It seemed perfect sense, and he began to wonder if this man spoke the truth. Had he been a fool to think that he could train as a knight and not become one?

"Who *are* you?" he asked.

The other man inclined his head as though he had won a victory.

"I am *you*, Faran. I am Knight Faran, a Kingshield Knight. I am all that you have trained so hard to become."

117

Even as he spoke the other man lifted up his helm and Faran saw his face. His own face. What the man had said was true, even if it seemed impossible.

Knight Faran placed the helm back on his head. "Do you know who you are, now?"

Faran was no longer sure of anything. The world seemed to have spun into mist and shadows.

"I see that you do not, so I will tell you. You are Faran that was. Even as we speak all that you have become fades away from you, and you will become what you always should have been. Not a knight, but a hunter. And the village, and Ferla whom you abandoned, will be as they were. But for that to happen, you must die first. For you failed Dromdruin and Ferla both."

Knight Faran drew his sword, and the blade rested lightly in his hands. It was clear that he had the skill to use it.

Faran swiftly raised his own, but he felt a pang of fear. His other self was right, but how could he beat him in a duel? He knew everything he did, and was equally as skilled.

Something else troubled him. He seemed to remember Kareste giving him a warning, but that memory was lost as the knight stepped forward.

Faran retreated a few steps, delaying what he knew was inevitable.

"You said Ferla is here. But what of the Ferla that trained with me as a knight?"

"That Ferla is soon to die. She will die because you left her, but the Ferla you once knew lives. Not the seventh knight Ferla, but the hunter Ferla. To reunite with her, all that you have become must die."

The knight circled him on cat's feet, looking for a weakness. Then he struck swiftly, moving into Tempest Blows the Dust.

Faran followed a standard countermeasure and stepped back lightly into Serpent Recoils. The knight's whirlwind attack ebbed, and Faran struck forward in a vicious stab.

The knight retreated in turn, and a soft laughter came from within the helm.

"You can do nothing that I cannot foresee, and this is a fight you cannot win."

They both attacked at the same time then, and steel rang against steel as their blades flashed through the air. All around them people came out of houses and cottages. They were people Faran knew. He had known them his whole life, but a part of him, deep at the back of his mind, remembered how he had last seen them. Dead, and burned in flames.

Something was wrong here, but he had no time to think of what. A mighty blow descended at his head, and he retreated to avoid it. He was too quick for his opponent, but even as he thought that he realized his helm was gone. It had not fallen off. It had simply vanished and left him vulnerable.

Knight Faran laughed softly again, and the sound was void of humor as it issued from beneath the helm he still wore.

Again the knight attacked, this time in Running Hare Changes Course. Faran stepped to the side and struck a blow, but it was too slow and his opponent merely swiveled and came after him again.

Once more their swords clashed and sparks flew from the blades. It was an inferior way of fighting. Deflections were better than blocks, but when the opponents were so evenly matched then brute force would come into play.

But suddenly Faran realized something. They were evenly matched in skill, but not in equipment. Not only was his helm gone, but now also his mail shirt. One thrust

119

of his enemy's blade, if it struck him, was sure to kill him now.

On the fight went. Knight Faran was implacable. He fought with relaxed grace and ease. Almost, he looked casual, moving from pose to pose in a deadly dance where at any moment his blade might bring death.

Yet Faran withstood him. Without helm or armor he held his own, but that was not enough. It would never be enough. How could he win against such an opponent?

The fight wore on, and the crowd watched silently. Faran knew he was missing something here, something vitally important but he was too busy staying alive to think about it. If he lost concentration for but a moment, he would die.

With a wild cry that was out of character the knight lunged. Faran skipped back out of the way, but he still felt the tip of his enemy's sword snick him. Nearly, he had died.

Knight Faran did not pursue him. Rather, he leaned on his sword as though it were a staff and spoke again, his hollow voice laden with authority.

"The end draws near, Faran. Soon you will be dead, and you can return to what was and what should have been."

"You know something?" Faran replied. "You talk too much. I don't think you're really me at all. And you're just as much at risk of being killed as I am."

The knight laughed once more, and it seemed genuine this time and carefree.

"You think you are a chance of killing me? Tell me this, then. How do you intend to do that without a sword?"

Faran did not understand, but even as he lifted up his sword arm he felt that it was suddenly light. His sword was gone.

Cold fear stabbed through him. How was this possible. He was defenseless now against an enemy intent on killing him.

He wanted to run, but that was not in him. Enemies had to be faced, if possible. But how?

There was no more time to think. Knight Faran began to advance again, and he was the image of a warrior intent on killing. He moved with grace and certainty, his sword tip held before him, his steps slow and careful, the dark gaze behind the helm hard to see but radiating confidence.

Faran stepped back, but he did not flee. Asana had taught him ways that an unarmed man might defeat a swordsman, but he had also said the chances of success were low.

The knight lashed out, his sword flashing in a silver arc through the twilight air, and it whistled faintly as it slashed just before Faran's throat.

But Faran was not there. He knew what stroke was coming before it had been launched, and he had stepped back and to the side. But he dared not close in to try to disarm his opponent.

Knight Faran gazed at him mockingly. "The end is near, now."

Faran watched, and a sense of helplessness overtook him. It was not his way to give up, and he would not. If he must, he would close with his opponent bare hands against a sword. But there could be little hope of victory that way.

He stepped back and to the side, forcing his opponent to react. Even as Knight Faran moved Faran leaped in toward him, trying to catch him off balance. But the blade came up in a glittering arc and nearly tore out his throat. He only just twisted out of the way in time, and then he reeled back, vulnerable himself.

But the knight did not press home his advantage. It was the first mistake he had made, and Faran did not understand why. It was not one he would have made.

The knight slowly advanced, but something had changed. Faran felt his strung bow over his shoulder, and a quiver of arrows at his back. Surely they had not been there before. He did not know what was happening, and the strange feeling came back to him again that not all was what it seemed here. Yet he had one last real opportunity to survive this fight, and he took it.

He nocked an arrow, drew the bow and loosed it again as swift as thought. It was not hard. Before he learned the skills of a knight he was a hunter of great skill.

Nor did he miss his mark. The arrow sped home and buried itself in the throat of his opponent, stopped from going clear through only by the vertebra or even perhaps the lower part of the back of the skull.

Knight Faran jolted into the air, then fell, but by the time he hit the ground he faded away like smoke on the wind. Faran looked, amazed that this had happened but grateful not to see his own dead body.

He looked up, and walking down the street toward him was Ferla. She was dressed as she always used to be, in hunter's garb. She carried a bow but no sword, and she was smiling at him.

He was struck by her beauty. Her long red hair trailed behind her, dark in the deepening evening. Her every movement was a blend of feminine grace and the athleticism of a hunter used to roaming the wild woods. Now, he could tell her he loved her as he always wanted to. He could live the life that had been taken from him.

Yet even as he thought that, he also remembered Ferla as the seventh knight. He remembered her on Nuril Faranar and in the valley of the lake. She was out there somewhere, and she was real. This was illusion, for there could not be two such as her. To stay here was to abandon reality for a dream, and to deny what he himself had become. He was a hunter no more, but a knight.

Light tore at his eyes. Tears ran down his face, and he reeled and spun like a leaf on the winds of a storm.

18. A Dark Night

Menendil led the other two men through the nighttime streets of Faladir, but their journey felt different to anything he had ever experienced in the city before.

Caludreth and Norgril were close behind, but they had taken their turn at leading too. Some of the streets were still deep in snow. It had not melted, and they followed the least used ways to conceal themselves, and those ways had not been well cleared.

Knee deep in snow, pushing forward to forge a path for the others, Menendil still kept a keen watch of all around him. The snow was difficult, but it was not dangerous. Night Fliers were though, but they had seen none despite it being the middle of the night.

That was just as well. He had no desire to ever see one again, but it was no great relief. Night Fliers were not the only threat. There were said to be other creatures on the prowl, and there was always the danger of the king's soldiers as well.

Menendil began to tire. The snow was very deep here, for it was a back alley and seldom used, but he pushed forward. He had only taken over a little while ago and despite the difficulty he would not give in to it.

He breathed a sigh of relief though as they left the alley and came on to a larger street. The snow had been cleared here by shovels and thousands of feet, and it was only ankle deep. But despite that good turn of luck, it was more dangerous in its way.

They moved ahead, more in the open now than they had been and more visible. Their luck held and there was no sign of any living thing out here with them, although at times they heard voices drifting to them from some of the buildings. Even that was rare though, for the night was old and most people were sleeping.

They came to a part of the city that Menendil did not know so well, and the buildings were less grand and the streets narrower. Almost, Menendil thought of it as the poor quarter of Faladir, but he knew better.

Despite the looks of the place, there was money here. Perhaps more so than in the old parts of the city close to his inn where the obviously rich and the nobles dwelt. This was the industrial center of the city, and there were factories of craftsmen here producing sterling work in wood, metal and jewels that ended up being sold not just throughout all of Faladir but all of Alithoras. Although truly wealthy individuals were rare here, as a group these workers were the best off in all of the city, and their homes, though looking nondescript from the outside were often luxurious in the interior.

Caludreth led the way now, for he knew this part of the city better. But their luck had finally run out, and ahead of them in the dark they saw the sudden swinging of several lamps and the tread of many booted feet as a patrol of soldiers turned a corner and came into view.

"Quickly," hissed Caludreth. "We walked past an alley just a moment ago."

They turned back and retraced their steps hurriedly. It was only fifty feet behind them, but Menendil felt completely exposed. There was no cover here at all.

Norgril darted into the darker opening of the alley, and the others followed. There, they looked back where they had come from.

The soldiers were getting closer now, and their lanterns seemed bright against the dark, but there was no sign that they had seen the three men hiding from them. They marched ahead, neither slower nor faster than before, and they talked among themselves as they did so.

Menendil knew what had protected the three of them. The lanterns had ruined the night sight of the soldiers, and though they could see well in the area immediately around them, their vision of things beyond that ring of light was muted.

Caludreth drew them a little deeper into the alley. The snow was deeper here, but a path had been worn through it right in the middle. It was narrow though, and if they had to run it would still be slow going.

They stilled and crouched low as light flared bright at the mouth of the alley. The soldiers had paused and gathered there, and the brick walls of the buildings took up their voices and cast them back and forth strangely.

The soldiers seemed curious about something. Menendil worried that he and his companions had been seen despite his earlier thinking that they had not. Then he realized several of the shadowy figures stooped low as if to look at something. They had, perhaps, seen fresh tracks in the snow.

"Come out!" thundered a voice. It would be the captain of the patrol.

Menendil did not move. Nor did Caludreth or Norgril. They remained just as they were, but he knew his two friends, just like him, were ready to run the moment the soldiers set foot in the alley.

The soldiers seemed divided, and they appeared to be disputing a point. But after a few moments Menendil heard someone speak disgustedly.

"There's no one there. We're wasting our time."

To this, there seemed to be some agreement, for shortly afterward the soldiers took up their march again and disappeared.

For a while, the three companions remained motionless.

"It could be a trap," Caludreth whispered.

Menendil agreed. The soldiers might have gone, or they might just have moved away and now be waiting nearby to see if anyone came out of the alley. Worse, it was possible the captain had sent men around to guard the exit on the other end. If so, the three of them would be cornered here.

Menendil made a decision. "We're going out ahead, no matter what. And we're doing it now."

He stood and drew his sword. The others did likewise, nor did they debate his decision. They had calculated the same possibilities as he had.

Menendil moved forward. He walked softly, so as to make no noise, but he did not walk slowly. It would not take long for men to come up behind if that was what was being planned.

He reached the mouth of the alley, and there he hesitated. This was the moment of greatest danger. He strained to hear anything, or to see some glimmer of lantern light in the distance, but nothing was out of place.

With a quick step, and his sword held high, he came out onto the larger street and looked around. He saw nothing, and heard nothing except the rapid breathing of his two companions. They were ready for a fight, and he realized his own breathing was heavy and his heart thudded.

The soldiers were gone though, and he breathed a sigh of relief. Without speaking, he sheathed his blade and led them forward on their quest once more. They had escaped, and their luck really had held, but the night's work was only just beginning.

They walked the streets abandoned at night by the sane folks of the city. Only soldiers patrolled in the dark, and only the foolish or the drunk walked the shadowy ways between buildings. And the desperate who preyed upon them for coin. Anyone met was not a friend, but an enemy.

Menendil added to his list of soldiers, fools and drunks. Patriots dared the city after dark as well, although it was certainly true that many would put them under the heading of fools.

They watched the skies too, for not all enemies walked on two feet, but they saw no sign of elù-draks at all. It occurred to Menendil that this might not be good news. What if they had been sent to find and kill the seventh knight?

It was something he had not really thought of before. He knew that the king was seeking the seventh knight, but he had not considered what that would be like. He fought against the king in his own way, but he was anonymous. The king did not know who he was, and had no real way to find him. So the king could not direct forces against him.

It was not so with the seventh knight. The king knew, at least down to the two young fugitives under Aranloth's care that Caludreth had met, who the seventh knight was and where they had last been seen. Given that the prophecy signaled the greatest threat to the king's plans was one of these, he would direct all his dark might against them. Elù-draks, knights, soldiers, perhaps even whole armies and who knew what other creatures of the dark would be hunting them? What hope did they have to survive that? What chance to even reach Faladir let alone somehow save it?

It was a depressing way of viewing the situation, but that did not make it less real. In truth, it was nearly beyond hope that the seventh knight would prevail, but dark times called for faith in hope more than any other time.

They turned a corner and came to a wide street with a slight downward slope. It was long, disappearing into the dark. Menendil was not sure if he had ever been down it before, but he had certainly stood on this corner several times, in his youth. He believed though that they had reached the right place.

Caludreth was more certain. "We are here, men. The right side of the street is mostly given over to smithies and workshops. The left to warehouses. Grain, unless things have changed, is usually kept in the first dozen or so warehouses on the left from the corner down."

They had discussed the probability of guards. Each warehouse would have at least one, for there was valuable property inside. They would have a means of summoning help too, if they saw suspicious activity. This would most likely be by the sounding of a horn.

They moved down the street, and as they did so Caludreth muttered. How he did it, Menendil did not know, for magic was a mystery to him, but the shadows deepened around them, and even walking so close together it became hard to see one another.

They moved quickly, for Caludreth had told them he did not have the strength to maintain the spell for long. The once-knight led them, and he chose the fifth building on the left as their target. Menendil and Norgril stayed close to him, for the darkness he had summoned dissipated within a few feet of his body.

The front door was close. It was a construction of two massive halves, big enough to allow the passage of wagons, each swinging on great posts of oak. As they suspected, a guard was positioned there. He was not easy to see, for he stood a little away from the door in the shadow of the eaves of the building, but they spotted him and skulked quietly down the side of the building. They had not expected to get in by the front way.

They stopped halfway down the side. There would be a back entrance, no doubt, but it was likely guarded too. Caludreth let slip the spell, and Norgril removed the small pinch bar that was looped to his belt. He wasted no time, and used the crooked end to find a gap between the weatherboards. Then, slowly, he used leverage to pull at the board.

It did not budge, and Norgril used more force. This was a moment of danger, for the more force that was used the less control he had and the greater chance of noise.

There was a slight wrenching sound as a nail was pulled part way out. Norgril paused, then readjusted his position and pulled again. This time he did so more softly, but the board began to come free.

Menendil and Caludreth knew what to do. They each gently cradled the board as it came free, and slowly placed it on the ground. It was a length of timber some fifteen feet long, but it only opened a gap a few inches high.

They looked in through the crevice, but they could see nothing of what was inside. They would have to enter, and for that they needed to remove more boards.

The minutes ran past quickly in the dark, and the tension in the air grew. But eventually there was enough of a gap to squeeze through, and with a final look around to ascertain that they had not been observed, they went inside.

Caludreth had told them he could summon light once inside, but there was always the chance of a guard stationed within the building, so they had decided not to risk that. Instead, they crept forward in the dark until they came to a long row of objects. It was not far in, and once close they felt that they were bags.

Caludreth cursed softly under his breath. "Likely grain," he whispered.

With a deft movement of his knife Menendil slashed one of the bags open. There was a soft sound and something poured quietly to the floor. He reached out with his hand and felt the running grains between his fingers.

"Let's get out," Menendil said. "This is not the warehouse we want."

This setback was not unexpected, but Menendil cursed it bitterly. It would be easier by far to just set alight this building. It was large, and news of the fire would spread all over the city. But they could not risk the chance that the king would let the people starve.

They tried another building, a few more down the road, but it too was stacked deep with bags of grain. It was a bad sign, for this was surely more than the king normally stored. And if he wanted, he could requisition the private stores of grain as well. Such a thing he would do if he needed to feed an army, and there was no one in the city who could stop him.

Their next break in, achieved by the use of Caludreth's spell as had been all the others, was far more successful. It was again several buildings down the street, and like the others had been guarded. They were getting good though at moving silently within their shadow, peeling away some weatherboards and gaining entry quickly.

"Look at this," whispered Caludreth, finally daring a weak spell that gave off a faint light. There were rows of empty barrels, and though they could see virtually nothing they felt the hilts of more than a dozen swords in each one.

A stronger light sprang up around them. "We need to see what we're doing here," Caludreth whispered.

Despite the risk, that was true. They would need to start several fires and to do it quickly. That way there was less chance of it being put out. To do this, they needed light.

Menendil looked around. He could still see only but dimly, but there were thousands of swords stored here, and masses of helms, chainmail coats, spears and bows. They had found what they were looking for, and they wasted no more time.

They each had tinderboxes and a small store of kindling. They lit multiple fires in places where the flames had access to walls and shelves. The place was lighting up fast and the fires catching on everywhere by the time they raced back toward the opening they had made in the wall. Their tinderboxes and the pinch bar were discarded. They would not need them anymore.

Smoke began to roil around them, but the light was growing bright quickly and with dread Menendil saw that their way out through the wall was blocked.

Before them stood a beast. At first, he thought it was a dog, but no dog was ever that big, and a deep rumbling came from its throat while the eyes glimmered in the firelight, blue and coldly menacing with human intelligence.

"A were-beast!" Caludreth cried, and even as he did Menendil recalled the legends he had heard of the elù-haraken, and more recently the strange rumors that had floated around the city.

But neither legend nor rumor prepared him for the reality of the beast before him. Wrongness radiated from it, and a sense of evil that was almost overpowering just by its presence. Dark sorcery had created this thing, and evil hung over it like a cloud.

Menendil looked behind it. Escape was so close, but the creature had set itself in their way and either it or all of them would die before anyone escaped the building that was fast turning into an inferno of leaping flames and twisting smoke.

19. Deep Into Darkness

Faran staggered out of the wall of light, and he would have fallen if Kareste had not been there to steady him.

"Faran!" she said. "Are you all right?"

The room seemed to spin around him, but she put an arm about his shoulders and held him steady.

"I'll be fine," he said after a moment.

It was a lie though. It had wrenched his heart to leave Ferla behind. Perhaps it was not real. He understood now that it was the magic of this room that had taken him to some other place. But it *might* have been real, in its way. And he yearned with all his heart to see her again as she was, as their lives could once have been, and as they could have lived them out together in happiness and peace in the home of his youth. The home, at least in the reality the magic had created, that had not been destroyed and where the occupants of his village had not been murdered.

He straightened, and Kareste removed her arm. "What *was* that magic?" he asked. "Was any of it real?"

She shook her head. "No. None of it was real. It is illusion, but it tests us all in different ways. Usually with fear." She eyed him closely. "Perhaps in your case it was with another emotion."

"Regret," he said simply.

Kareste looked at him earnestly, but she did not ask what illusions he had seen. He guessed it was the custom of this place not to speak of them, and he was certain that she would not reveal how she herself had been tested.

"Let's get away from here," he said. "I'm over this room, and the magic it contains."

She did not argue. No doubt they could both do with a rest, but the sooner they moved ahead the sooner they could help Aranloth and be out of here. He wanted to see the outside world again, and feel the sunlight on his face. Most of all, he wanted to see Ferla, but he began to wonder if he ever would again.

They left the chamber behind them, and the way ahead was a single tunnel. It was, Faran thought, not so much a tunnel as a shaft. He had heard that in mines there were passageways such as these. They descended at a steep angle to get deep, deep inside the earth, and that was what this one did. He certainly was glad to be descending it rather than climbing it.

There were no bodies here, either of the ancient Letharn or the initiates who sought to become wizard-priests. Likely the magic in the wall of light was the last test they faced.

It seemed to him that it grew warmer, but he was not sure. Why that should be deep in the earth, he did not know. Although he did recall Aranloth telling him once about rivers of molten stone deep in the earth that sometimes erupted into the world above. Perhaps they were near to a place such as that.

"This does not seem like the rest of the tombs," he said to Kareste. "What is this place?"

The lòhren did not slow her pace, but she answered promptly.

"I'm not sure, exactly. Aranloth never told me, but we're getting close to our destination now. This is where the death-sleep occurs. At least, the best place for it."

They walked on, and Faran felt the weight of the earth above press down on his mind. So too the weight of mysteries. What, exactly, was the death-sleep? Had Kareste herself used it? Was she older than she looked?

135

As was the way with lòhrens, Kareste rarely volunteered information on such subjects. He could ask, but he knew in advance that she would evade his questions. He was not ready for that knowledge. He was not a lòhren, and the lòhrens, though they gave much information out freely, held some secrets back. He understood why. Knowledge could be both a power and a burden. If it were granted before a person was ready they would not use it wisely. That was why Aranloth had not taught the knights the deeper secrets of magic. It was also why they were dangerous, for they gained power from the Morleth Stone but did not fully understand the nature of that power.

They continued downward, and there was no doubt in Faran's mind at all now that it was warmer. Even just touching the wall he felt the heat radiating from it.

"Is it safe here?" he asked.

"Nowhere is safe in the tombs," came the answer.

That much he knew already, but there was something different here. He could sense it. Uneasiness grew in him, even if he could not quite identify its source. There was magic nearby. He knew that, but it was of more than one kind.

The tunnel took a gradual curve to the left. This was not normal in the tombs. Usually, there were direct corners or crossroads. Why it should be different here was strange, but perhaps the ancient builders had wanted to avoid something.

He had no more time to think about that though. Abruptly, Kareste came to a stop. She held up her staff and the light at its tip flared brighter. Her head was cocked to one side though, as if in curiosity.

Whatever it was that she sensed, he felt it too. It was something strangely familiar, and it was the source of the magic that he had sensed earlier.

Even as they came to a standstill, something emerged from the shadows ahead. It was a tall figure, clothed in white, and it walked forward leaning on a staff.

Kareste hissed. "Aranloth?"

"Why can you not just let me be?" the lòhren asked her. "My time is done, and I deserve to rest."

The figure came into the light. It *was* Aranloth, though he seemed haggard and blood seeped into his robes from many wounds over his body.

20. Snow Warriors

The growl of the were-beast was chilling. It made no move, but it had them. There was but one escape from the growing flames behind the three companions, and the beast blocked them from it.

The creature must have tracked them here, perhaps having first discovered their entry into one of the other buildings.

Norgril dashed to the right, trying to distract it, but the creature merely swiveled its great head and watched him. It made no move away from the exit in the wall.

"We'll have to fight it," Caludreth said, and he drew his great sword.

The creature moved then, and Menendil had the terrible feeling that it had understood the words just spoken.

It leaped for Caludreth's throat, and it was stunning that something that large could move so fast. But the once-knight was ready, and he dodged to the side swinging his sword in a great arc to kill the creature.

The were-beast turned in mid jump though, ensuring it only caught a glancing blow from the blade. It landed, rolled, and leaped again.

Caludreth tried a thrust this time, but one of the massive paws of the beast swiped his blade aside. Menendil was moving now, and he came in from the side with his own thrust.

The creature danced backward. It was no longer between them and the way of escape, but to turn their backs on it was to die. They had no choice but to keep fighting.

Norgril bent and picked up the pinch bar that he had discarded earlier, and he flung it with all his might at the great hound. It struck the creature on the shoulder, but the beast did not move. Its only reaction was to growl, and the hackles along its neck and upper back rose.

Caludreth charged it, his sword swirling in figure eights before his body. Norgril came in from one side, and Menendil danced around to the other. They had to trap this thing between them.

The hound backed up. But the flames had begun to roar behind it. With a sinking feeling Menendil knew they were running out of time here. A hue and cry might already have gone up, and soon the streets would be swarming with activity as guards tried to put out the fire or protect the neighboring warehouses. How could they escape with all that going on?

The were-beast had backed away as far as it could. The heat from the flames was becoming intense, and even Menendil felt it strongly and he was not so close.

Suddenly, the creature swiveled to its right and went for Norgril. Quicker than thought it leaped for him, paws slashing and the great jaws snapping. The sword was swept out of his friend's hands, and Menendil cried out and ran forward to help, but he knew he would be too late.

Somehow Norgril managed to roll and bring up his shoulder to protect his neck, though he cursed as the teeth bit deep into his flesh. A moment later Caludreth was there, and his sword hacked down. It took the beast on its spine, and there was a loud crack as bones shattered.

The creature spun around and snapped at the sword, wrenching it from Caludreth's hand. Then the thing leaped at him.

Had it been unwounded, it would have jumped at Caludreth's neck, but its back legs gave out from under it and it only reared up waist high.

Menendil reached it then, but he could deliver only a glancing blow for he was afraid of hitting his friend. Yet Caludreth caught the beast, one hand around its neck and another around a hind leg. All in one motion, even as the hound tried to bite away his hand, Caludreth wheeled and hurled the beast back into the warehouse and amid the roiling flames and smoke.

"Quickly!" Menendil cried. "Out through the wall!"

Norgril was first through, and then Caludreth. Menendil came last, but he staggered into his friend's back, for the once-knight had come to an unexpected standstill.

Menendil soon saw why. They were surrounded. Somehow, a dozen of the king's soldiers were there. They had probably followed the were-beast. The warehouses were better guarded than expected, and that error was now going to cost them dearly. There could be no escape from this. There could only be death or capture, and death was by far more preferable. That way, at least, they could protect those that knew them.

A soldier stepped forward, and Menendil knew from the markings on his uniform he was a captain.

"You are caught, at last," the man said. "Did you think the king would ignore rebels? He has all places watched, and you have walked into our trap."

"Rebels?" Caludreth said. "We are not rebelling, but patriots. The king is the rebel, and the seventh knight will bring justice to this realm. If you are lucky, you will live to see it. But I think your luck has run out, this night."

The captain stared hard, and in the light of the leaping flames from the building behind them, Caludreth's face was plain to see.

The captain stepped back and gasped. "It's him! It's the traitor knight!"

The soldiers were surprised, and Caludreth used that momentary shock to advantage and attacked them. The great sword swept out, and the captain's head flew through the air. Blood spurted from the open neck, arcing high into the air and disappearing. Then the body toppled, but the blood still leaped out.

Menendil unleashed a battle cry, and tore into the enemy. Nothing would save him or his friends here, for they were outnumbered. But the skills of Caludreth had given them the slightest chance. He had created surprise, and then deprived the men of leadership. With luck, that would disconcert the soldiers and cause panic.

Swiftly, Menendil thrust with his sword, and felt the tip bite home into chainmail. It was not a killing blow, but the soldier reeled back and stumbled into a companion.

Norgril was among them now too, his sword flashing in desperate arcs. He killed one man, and went for another. But this man deftly blocked the strike meant to kill him and flicked his blade back in a counterattack. Norgril only just managed to avoid it.

Menendil was busy too, driving forward and slashing at another man. He retreated, but there was no sign the soldiers were going to break and flee.

Of Caludreth, there was no sign. He had fallen behind them, but suddenly his voice rose up and he uttered a spell. Menendil felt the hair on the back of his neck prickle. A sudden wind tore into them all, and the snow on the ground was picked up and flung around.

Menendil hacked at a blade thrust at him, and he not only blocked the blow but ran his own blade down his opponent's and twisted at the end to dislodge the weapon from him. He was about to step forward and strike again, when he saw a new warrior join the fray. It was a man of snow, a blade of ice in his hand, and he hacked and thrust. Suddenly there were more of the snow warriors, and the soldiers broke and fled, but one, even as he ran, turned back and cast a knife that struck Menendil hard. It hit him in the stomach and pierced deeply before dislodging when Menendil fell back onto the ground. He clasped his hand to the wound, and it was already wet with blood.

It took a few moments for the pain to start, but once it did it ripped through Menendil and he knew this was the worst wound he had ever received. If it did not kill him soon, then infection might.

21. The Abyss

The figure of Aranloth ceased hobbling toward them, and leaned upon his staff.

"Why do you wish to trouble me? Can you not leave me in peace?"

"Aranloth!" Faran cried out. "It's so good to see you. But you're hurt, let us help you!"

He went to move forward but Kareste gripped his shoulder, and her fingers sunk in like iron pincers.

"Wait," she commanded.

"But he's wounded!"

Even as Faran spoke, Aranloth stumbled and went down on one knee.

"He needs us!" Faran cried out again and tried to break free, but Kareste's grip was unrelenting.

"Wait!" she commanded again, and there was such power in her voice that Faran ceased to struggle.

Aranloth looked at them from his haggard face, and fresh blood seeped into his white robes. The staff on his hand tumbled forward and rattled against the stone floor.

No one moved. The only sound was the harsh breathing of the old man. Then slowly, he stood, and he did not use the staff. In fact, Faran saw it vanish from sight as if it had never been.

The old man changed as they watched. Instead of one figure, he seemed to separate like smoke blown in a breeze, and three figures now stood there. They were women, stern faced and proud. Fire gleamed in their eyes, and their mouths were twisted in a silent hiss.

"The harakgar," muttered Faran, and he was ashamed that he had been taken in by their ruse. Had Kareste not held him back from going to help, he would now be dead. But he sensed that she had not been sure either.

Yet she was now, and her voice rang out full of confidence and power.

"Har nere ferork. Skigg gar see!"

It was the charm that subdued the Three Sisters, the only power that availed against them, and their faces contorted at the words.

With a scream they rushed forward, half running and half flying, but they did not close on the two intruders in the tombs. Instead, they turned into plumes of smoke and rose up to the ceiling and seeped into the stone.

Faran trembled, and he realized his sword was in his hand. He sheathed it and cursed himself. The blade was no use against the magic that guarded this place. It had been instinct to draw it, but it was the wrong reaction here. Only the charm held power.

"A close call," Kareste muttered. "But time presses and we must go on."

She did not rebuke him for his mistake, and he was grateful for that. She knew, as well as he, that it was not one he would make again.

Time seemed to have lost meaning as they pressed ahead. Faran felt tired, but not badly. If they needed to rest, they could do it in turns and keep a watch, but it would be better to find Aranloth and escape as soon as possible.

The passageway they followed began to zig zag back and forth, but it ever descended at a steep angle. How deep in the earth they were, he did not wish to think about. Yet the air still seemed fresh enough to breathe, and there was no sign that this part of the underground system was ever used or even intended for burials.

144

The tunnel, in fact, only seemed to have one purpose and one destination. That was to reach down deep into the bowels of the earth.

It was no longer warm. Faran felt the walls at times, and they had returned to a normal temperature. But something else had taken the warmth's place as a background feeling. Magic. It was of a kind that Faran had never felt before, or maybe his growing skills were only now good enough to detect it. He had been to the tombs before, but maybe last time he had not been sensitive enough. Whatever the case, that feeling grew.

From time to time, Kareste called a halt. She was wary of the harakgar, but something else seemed to be troubling her as well. Once more, Faran got the sense that she was holding something back, but he could not be sure. They did not talk much, even during these brief rests.

Eventually, the tunnel changed. It still descended, but not so steeply. Nor did it cut back and forth, but now ran straight ahead.

"We are close now," Kareste told him. "Prepare yourself."

She did not say exactly what he should prepare himself for. That Aranloth was dead? Certainly, that was a possibility. They both knew it. Yet it might refer to the harakgar too. Maybe they would seek to strike again when those they guarded against would be distracted. Or maybe she meant something entirely different.

Abruptly, the left wall of the tunnel simply ceased to exist.

"Walk warily," Kareste instructed. "This place is dangerous."

He could see why. Where the wall had been a vast chasm opened up. He glanced downward, but its bottom, if there even was one, was lost in the dark. Although he did think he saw a glimmer of light come and go

145

somewhere in those unfathomable depths. He chose not to look down anymore. Heights disturbed him, and he stuck close to the wall on the right and watched only his feet as they trod warily on the narrow path.

It was slow going. Kareste was in a hurry, and he knew why. But here, she took each step carefully and led the way forward as though a misstep could mean death. Which was only the truth.

Faran was not sure if Aranloth had followed this route himself or if he had come some other way, if there even was one. But the thought of him struggling down this narrow path, with the chasm a step away and waiting to swallow him, while wounded close to death, wrenched at his heart. How much could one man endure?

To his left, there was a sudden gleam of lights in the abyss. Like fish in a lake the lights rose, turned and flashed away again. What they were, he did not know. He did remember seeing their like on his first journey through the tombs though. But whatever they were, they were central to the magic that lay over this whole place.

They continued downward. The lights came and went more regularly now, and though there was something eerie about them, they did not disturb him in the way the harakgar did. Somehow, he sensed that the magics that bound them both were related, but they were different aspects of the same power. In some way, they were opposites. He wished he understood magic better, but this was beyond him. He suspected it was beyond even many lòhrens.

The pathway began to level out. It seemed they had gone as deep as they were going to. The lights rose and flashed close now, and the path even began to widen a little.

Kareste's staff no longer gave off any light. When she had withdrawn that little magic, he did not know. Yet there was ample light now by which to see.

The path widened into a kind of shelf, and Kareste came to a standstill.

"We are here," she said.

Faran looked around. Apart from the lights, he saw nothing.

"I don't see him," Faran replied. "Where's Aranloth?"

She raised her staff and pointed. "Out there."

He could not believe it. "You mean in the abyss? How is that even possible?"

"He rides the magic, and it binds and secures him. He is one with it, and it protects him."

She moved cautiously farther out on the ledge. Faran followed her, and he could not believe what he saw. Aranloth was below, suspended by a gathering of those mysterious lights, and he hung in the chasm, nothing to support him from falling into the endless dark but light. He hung in it like a man resting in a hammock.

The old man seemed asleep. His staff was gathered in the crook of an arm, and his eyes were closed, but he did not move, nor could Faran even detect the slightest rise and fall of his chest. It was more than sleep. It looked as if his body was somehow empty.

"Are we too late?"

Kareste did not answer, and when he looked at her he saw that her eyes were closed. He thought this was grief, but then he sensed some subtle manifestation of her magic. It reached out and probed the strange scene before them.

"He is dead," Kareste said, opening her eyes. "In all the ways that count. Yet the death of the death-sleep is not irrevocable. The magic that healed his body preserves it also. If his spirit can be brought back to it swiftly, he will live."

"How do we do that?" Faran asked.

She turned her gaze upon him, and there was deep emotion, so often hidden but now momentarily revealed, in her green-brown eyes. He could not fathom what she was feeling, but regret was a part of it.

22. A Spirit Quest

"I cannot do it, Faran. You must bring Aranloth back, if it can be done at all. You must travel the void as you did once for Ferla, and return his spirit to his body even as you did her."

That was not what Faran was expecting, and he felt his heart thrash in his chest. If there was a place worse than the tombs, it was the void, and fear coursed through him.

He understood at last what Kareste had been holding back from him. He had known she harbored a secret, and this was it, finally revealed.

"Are you not better suited to travel the void than I am?" he asked.

"I am," she answered.

"Then why do you not go?"

"Think about it, Faran."

He realized instantly what she meant, and despite that she had held this information back from him, for surely she must have guessed this from the beginning, he had sympathy for her. He knew she would take the role of greatest danger if she could, and that it hurt her to ask of him what she did.

"The magic to go, or to send someone, to the void is great. It is a skill beyond me. So you must do that, and I must be the one sent."

She nodded. "It is one of the great magics, and it is beyond even most lòhrens. It is not beyond you though. One day, you will achieve such skill. But that is years ahead of you, yet."

"But why did you hide this from me?"

She turned away. "I wish that I did not have to. Perhaps I was even wrong to do so. My belief was, and is, that the knowledge of this task would have weighed you down. The void is a dangerous place, as you know. Deadly. Few would survive what I ask of you, but you have done it before. I believe you can do it again. But to know all this in advance would be to burden you with fear and fill your mind with doubt. It might have prevented you from even attempting it. The long-held fear is worse than the sudden one."

"And if I say no, now?"

"Then Aranloth dies." She let those words hang in the air for several moments before she spoke again. "Even so, this is something I ask of you only. I cannot compel it, nor would I even if I could. Likewise, I'll not judge you if you say no. The choice is yours, and I do not begrudge it to you. Even I would fear to go."

Faran looked out into the chasm, and he felt lost. He looked at Aranloth, suspended by powers that were a mystery to him, and knew that he was out of his depth.

But he gave the only answer he could, or would want to.

"I will do it. At least, I'll make the attempt."

Kareste gave him a searching look. What she hoped to discern, he could not tell. Perhaps she wanted to know if he held anything against her for the knowledge she had withheld. He did not. She had made what she thought was a good choice, and her reasons were sound. Had he been plagued by fear all the way here, he would not be mentally strong now. She had served him well, in fact. For now, he wanted to do this thing. Only he could attempt it, and he owed it to Aranloth to try. Determination was growing in him, and time would not have an opportunity to erode it.

"How do we do it?" he asked.

"You must be near him, even as you were with Ferla. And I will lay my staff over the both of you to form a bridge of magic between the two of you."

He looked down at Aranloth, suspended in the abyss only by magic.

"But how can I even get there?"

"Trust the magic, Faran, and trust your eyes. Neither deceive you. The lights will support your weight. You need only step out there."

He glanced out into the chasm again. That was easy for Kareste to say, but doing it would require great strength of will. How could he know he would not plummet to his death?

Nevertheless, he trusted what she said. He got down on his hands and knees, and edged closer to the abyss. All he could do at first was let a foot drift out over the end of the rock platform, but as soon as he did so he saw the lights around Aranloth swirl and eddy. Some came toward his foot, and he felt a strange sensation as though his foot were supported by water. Only it was stronger.

He tried his hardest not to think of the chasm. But the more he tried not to think about it, the more it intruded on his mind. Yet he edged out farther, and the lights shifted and flowed around him.

Moving out even more, he was buoyed by the magic. It was a strange feeling, and the lights settled all around him. They supported him, and he began to trust the sensation, strange as it was.

"Stay close to Aranloth," Kareste warned.

Faran did so. He pushed out, losing contact with the stone ledge at last, and he hung, suspended by arcane powers that he did not understand, next to Aranloth. He was shoulder to shoulder with the lòhren, but looking up into the dark it did not feel so bad, and the fear of falling was gone. The magic would support him, and strange as it

151

was there was something comforting too. He almost felt as though the magic cooperated with him, and that it approved of what he was doing.

Kareste knelt down on the ledge. She placed her staff across his chest, and it reached over Aranloth's as well. Then she stood.

Faran had seldom seen her look so grim, but there was determination in the set of her jaw. He wondered how she would deal with the harakgar, and how she would find rest by herself if he did not return swiftly. But she was a lòhren, and she would have considered all these things herself. Yet still, he realized that he was not the only one taking risks here.

He sensed the power of magic well up in her, and then she spoke words of power. He did not know them, though he knew he had heard them before when Aranloth had once performed the same rite. He realized too that they were more than just words of power, but a spell of complexity. And the words were only one aspect. The magic was indeed deep, profound, and beyond his grasp. But he did get a sense of a reordering of the very powers that formed and substanced the world. It was a fleeting glimpse of something vast and structured, and that order having a new pattern embedded in it.

Then the staff grew heavy over his chest, and he remembered what would come next. Even as he thought it, the weight of the staff intensified. It felt like a tree across his body, and he could not draw breath.

"You go to a place of spirit," Kareste intoned, speaking now directly to him. Then she uttered more words of power, and the world darkened as though he slept.

"Be at peace. But remember! Come back by the way you go in. There is no other way. Remember!"

He drifted away in the dark, his consciousness dwindling like the last spark of a failed fire.

"Your mind is both armor and weapon." Kareste's voice faded away, and there was nothing now except the great dark. He drifted in an ocean of nothingness, and neither time nor form meant anything to him. The universe was vast, yet within the grip of his hand, but at the same time he was smaller than a grain of sand compared to the weight of the whole world.

For a while, which might have been an eternity or swifter than the flutter of his eyelids, there was nothing. Then his drifting in nothingness seemed to take him somewhere. First, he smelled the scent of old smoke. It hung in the air, stale and rank. Then the darkness gave way to a twilight world. He lay on gravelly ground, looking up. There was neither sun, nor moon nor stars. But the sky was lit by an orange glow as if great fires had burned the day before.

He sat up, and then stood. His spirit quest had begun, and it did not matter that his body ached and that he had a dull headache. He was in the void now, and this was no place to lie on the ground unwitting of enemies. He looked around, but saw nothing familiar.

This was not the way that he had entered before. There was no ravine, yet still there was a river of dark water that flowed sluggishly before him. By the shore was a boat. Small and well made, the once bright timber now darkened by the water which stained it black.

The way forward was clear enough. He must use the boat to cross the river, but he marked the spot as well. He must also come back this way.

He did not waste any time. The sooner he was done here, the better. He would not grow tired in the void, nor need sleep. But time was his enemy. The longer he was here the harder it would be to return, and the greater the chance of being attacked by the strange denizens of this hapless shadow world.

The boat moved easily over the water. There were two oars, but these he barely seemed to use. A few strokes were enough to glide him to the middle of the river. From there, he could see somewhat of the land beyond. Nothing seemed familiar to him, nor did he see any living thing. He was alone here, or so it seemed. But he did not trust that. Already he had the feeling that he was being watched.

A few more sweeps of the oars sent him on his way again, and the boat seemed to float on the dark water. He could feel the current below him in the timbers of the vessel, but it was as though it was far away and weak. Yet the boat sped across the surface like the insects he used to watch in the creek in Dromdruin. Water skimmers the villagers called them, and that brought back old memories.

The villagers were dead though, and beyond his recall. Yet Aranloth might live. That must be his only concern now, and reaching him safely. He had a vague sense of where he was. That was how the magic worked, and why the seeker was better to be a person who knew the lost spirit well. That connection was a link in the void.

He came to the opposite shore, and drew his boat well up on the bank. He did not suppose that any denizen here could harm it, or if they did that he could not summon another boat by the power of his mind, for the power of the will was paramount here, yet still he hid the boat within some tall grasses, seemingly dead, and hoped that it would not be found.

"Welcome to the void, little brother," came a voice.

Faran stepped back and drew his sword. There was no one visible though, but after a moment a Kingshield Knight stepped away from behind a gnarled and rotting tree farther along the bank.

"Sofanil," breathed Faran. It was all he could think to say for the presence of his enemy here dismayed him. How could this be?

154

"That is *Knight* Sofanil, to you."

Faran found his voice. "I am not your brother, still less a little one."

"Ah, but that is youth speaking, and the pride you might one day learn to suppress. At least, if you were to become a genuine knight and not a plaything of the lòhrens."

Faran resumed a more relaxed stance, but he did not lower his sword. Yet blades were not the only weapons in a fight. Words were too, but he had no intention of debating Sofanil's comments and falling into the trap of playing his game.

"Truly, I had not expected to see you here. What can I do for you? Do you need help?"

He spoke with a smile. This was a contest of words, and what he had said must surely be the last thing Sofanil expected to hear. Surprise was a game that two could play.

The knight raised an eyebrow, and a faint smile hovered over his lips.

"You are clever indeed. I see now why once the king thought you to be the seventh knight."

To that, Faran gave no answer. Did his opponent know that Ferla was the seventh knight? There was no likely reason for him to know that, so by keeping his silence the truth, and Ferla, might be protected.

"Oh, don't flatter yourself, boy. I know you're not the prophesied one. I know the truth, and all of it. So there is no need to try to deceive me. It is a riddle long solved by the king. But *this* riddle, see what you make of it and how long it takes you to solve!"

As Sofanil spoke he thrust out a hand and sorcery spurted from his fingers. Faran raised a shield, quick as thought, but the attack was not of fire. It was merely light, and on touching his magic shield it faded away to ash and was gone.

155

So too was Sofanil. Under cover of that light he had vanished, or the sending that he had sent to the void had, for flesh did not exist here.

But the mystery of what he had done remained.

23. A Throne of Skulls

The Morleth Stone was hot to touch. Sometimes it was cold. Often it seemed lighter or heavier than it looked. At whiles it gleamed with inner lights, yet on other occasions was dark as the pit.

Druilgar took these vagaries in his stride. What did its appearance or feel matter to him, so long as the magic was of benefit?

He held it now, clasped between his two palms and close to his chest, and its magic coursed through him. More and more of late he had been able to open himself to it. In the early days some part of him had resisted, but that blockage was now destroyed.

He sat within the upper chamber of the Tower of the Stone. But neither tower nor city nor realm meant anything to him now. He opened himself a little more, and felt the magic rush through him like a raging torrent. It was as a river in flood. It was like the swell of the ocean in a storm. It was like the fall of winter after summer was spent. It was inevitable and irresistible, and he loved it.

He wanted more.

More would never be enough. He wanted it all, even if it killed him. The stone had so much more to give. He knew that he had so far only tapped into a small portion of all it had to offer, and that it only eked out its power to him chafed. He cared nothing that such powers might kill him. Let them! But if they did not, he would become as a god.

The stone, though, while it gave him more all the time never took him past his limits. Perhaps it needed him as much as he needed it. Perhaps.

The flow of power slowed. He trembled all over, and the hair on his neck rose like hackles on a dog. He felt nauseous, and his heart thudded unevenly in his chest. He knew his life clung to his body by a thread, and he did not care.

But as the influence of the stone reduced, caution returned to him. It was ever thus. While the stone fed him power, he yearned for it. When it withdrew its benevolence, he became grateful for what it had given, and glad that he yet lived. He knew he might die any time he did this, and that terrified him as the sway of the stone over his mind lessened, but he could never stop himself from risking it all again. The pressure to do so built day by day until he was like a parched man desperate to drink lifegiving water.

This time, though, the stone was not done. He felt it cool in his hands, and though the power running through him had slowed to a trickle, some residue of magic lay over his mind, and it gave him a vision.

He knew immediately it was of the past. Armies battled, and men, elugs, elves, trolls, dragons, were-beasts and a hundred other creatures of the Light or the Dark contended against each other on green fields turned red. Lòhrens battled elùgroths, and magic filled the air until it thrummed with force like the heavens when a storm unleashes fury on the world. Life vied against death, and death became master.

He saw in this vision the Shadowed Lord himself, Elùdrath, stride over the land as a god, tall and prideful, death in his glance and a retinue of shadow creatures to strike fear into the hearts of the boldest of the brave.

Then his mind shifted, and a different scene played out. Elves marched. Thousands of them, coming over the northern mountains and spilling into Alithoras like rivers of light. One among them wore a crown, and his eyes pierced like the sun. This was Halath, and he led his people during their great exodus.

When the elves moved over the mountains, out of deep caves came dwarves, axes in their hands and battle cries on their lips. They joined the elves, and so too the races of humanity. But not all. Some from the south joined the Great Master and fought alongside elugs.

But the battles drew to an end. Life gained the mastery over death. Humanity swelled in triumph, settling lands and building cities. The creatures of the Shadow dispersed. Some died out. Others hid. These were hunted, but not all were found. In the dark places of Alithoras they found succor. The mountains hid them. Vast forests became their lair. Deep valleys they haunted like shadows, unseen and lost amid flashing streams and tumbled stones.

And Druilgar understood. He knew why these visions were shown him, and he gathered his magic to him and reached out over all the land. He called the creatures of the Dark to him. He showed them his face, and they saw he was a king of the Dark, crowned by gold and wreathed in the shadows of the Morleth Stone. He was one with them, and dominion over them was given him. He called, and he felt them stir. He felt them wake with the yearning for blood and revenge, and this he promised them. And they came.

The vision fell away, and he let his magic subside. He was tired, yet he felt triumphant. His army would grow, and the battles that had been fought long ago would be fought anew. Only this time there was no Halath. Nor would the elves leave their forest stronghold. The nations of humanity would fall, and he, Druilgar, would take their rule and crush their kings and queens. Emperor of the Dark he would become, and he would not rest until he trampled the world beneath his boots.

A wave of ecstasy rolled over him, but even as it peaked excruciating pain cut through him. It was often so with the Morleth Stone. What it gave was never without price, and he screamed in agony. But he felt himself change also.

His hair grew longer, and his skin paled and became more supple. His eyesight sharpened, and he felt stronger, more vibrant, younger than he had since the far-off days of his youth.

The pain receded, and his enhanced body trembled, but he paid it little heed. What occupied his mind was the image of the Morleth Stone. Even holding his eyes closed, he saw it. He knew he always would, and that it was imprinted upon him like writing graven in stone. Never again would he be without it, and he did not mind. It was a beautiful sight, and if it overlayed all that he ever saw the world would be a better place.

Just as its image was with him, so too was its magic. It was there at every beat of his heart and every breath. He felt invincible. That was how it should be, for he was one with the stone and the stone was one with him.

Druilgar sighed as the powers that had run through him diminished and the sorcery ebbed. He reverently placed the stone back on the pedestal that was now its resting place. The iron box of old lay discarded in a corner of the chamber.

As he put it back though he saw that the black surface was now streaked with crimson. Like blood it seemed, shimmering and vibrant. He realized that even as the stone had become a part of him, he had become a part of it, and he rejoiced.

160

But the stone was not done, and it spoke to him. Not mind to mind or by images as it had in the past, but the air of the chamber thrummed with its voice.

Destiny draws nigh, my son.

Druilgar was surprised, but he knew he should not have been. The Morleth Stone was the greatest magic in Alithoras. Nothing was beyond it.

"I am ready, Osahka. The land awaits my coming, and I will go to it and bring order and rule. No longer will there be nations, but one nation. No longer will there be rulers, but one ruler. No longer will there be laws, but one law. And that shall be my will, for I am supreme above others, and I understand better and see farther."

The stone spoke to him then, and told him many things that had been and might yet be. Then it showed him another vision. It was of himself, but younger than he was now, though it was in the future. A crown was upon his head, greater than Faladir's, and his eyes were black orbs like twin Morleth Stones.

But better than this, he sat upon a throne. And it was no ordinary throne fit for lesser kings. It was a throne of skulls, each one belonging to kings and queens and the blood of royalty. These were the remains of those whom he had conquered, and it was a fitting seat for an emperor of the Dark.

The once great Aranloth bowed before him, and whispered counsels in his ear while he held court. But the lòhren's eyes were black orbs also.

At his side, on a throne of silver, sat his queen. She who had been Ferla, and she gazed at him with adoration.

The Light has prophecies, Osahka spoke again, *but we of the Dark have our foreshadowings of the future. They are yours to grasp and to turn into reality.*

Druilgar nodded slowly, and the presence of the stone faded until he was alone. He would make these things come to pass. Yet there had been no sign in the vision of the fate of the young man called Faran, and he wondered what that meant.

24. I Have No Secrets

There was no further sign of Sofanil, and Faran moved out into the strange land of the void.

A mist came up off the river and widened across the desolate landscape. It felt clingy and strange, and there was a sense of magic to it. But there was no spell being cast. The void itself was a place of magic.

There was a path, faint but distinct, and Faran followed it. He did not know what direction it led. He had a feeling it was north, but this was just a guess. In a place that had no sun, were there any directions at all? It puzzled him, but he put the thought aside.

He could feel the presence of Aranloth, albeit only just, and that was the only direction he needed. The path went that way, and he followed it. But he did not let down his guard. Sofanil had already waylaid him, and he would not let it happen again.

Sofanil's magic troubled him though. What had the light done? Why had Sofanil not tried to press home his attack? They were disturbing questions, and Faran had no answers to them.

Time slipped by, but he was not sure how much. It could not be measured in the void. Yet the mist ebbed and flowed, and the path began to run uphill. But Faran paused. Ahead, in a thick patch of mist, someone walked toward him.

Faran drew his sword. He did not really need it here, for he knew in the void that his mind was a weapon itself. Should he wish it, he could summon to him any weapon or magic he wished, but the sword was familiar and felt comfortable in his hand.

The figure strode through the mists, and it was a knight. Nor just any knight, for most realms had an order of warriors that were elite, but a Kingshield Knight.

Faran held his breath, then when he realized he was doing so he forced himself to relax and breathe normally. Was this friend or foe? He had hopes for the former, but in the void the latter was the more likely.

The figure drew close, and halted. "Hail, grandson. You have achieved much since last we met."

Faran did not lower his sword, and the knight threw back his head and laughed. Then he removed his helm, and Faran saw that it was indeed his grandfather. In the void all deceptions were possible, but no creature of evil could mimic the good-natured gleam in the man's eyes. And if it tried, Faran felt that he could detect the deception. There was none here.

"You have come a long way indeed, and not just in weapons and magic but also in wisdom."

"I have had good teachers," Faran replied. "But by all that is holy, it's good to see you."

"It's good to see you too, my boy. Yet we had better talk while we walk, for time presses."

They moved ahead into the mist then, following the same path. It kept climbing, and the mist grew thicker.

"I don't like it," Faran said. "The mist should have been thicker by the river, but instead it deepens as we climb."

"Do not fear the mist. Fear that which may hide in it. But it thickens here for a reason. Ahead is a waterfall, though it is still far away. That is the origin of the fog rather than sorcery."

They kept climbing, and the way had become steep. It reminded Faran of somewhere he had been before, but it was different too. Yet when they came, at length, to the crest of a mighty hill, he turned to his grandfather.

"This is the hill on which the city of the ancient Letharn was built." He swept out his hand and pointed out into the fog that lay like an ocean below them. "Down there is the great escarpment, and the Tombs of the Letharn, and the waterfall you spoke of."

"It is so," his grandfather replied. "At least, this is the shadow of those places, spilling out into the void."

"But how is it possible? There are no buildings here? Where are the ruins?"

"The void is a shadow realm. It's an echo of reality. Nothing more. It's like the real world, but sometimes the details are not there. Like buildings."

Faran felt the presence of Aranloth, and he was somewhere close. They moved ahead, and Faran was eager. So far, the only enemy he had encountered was Sofanil. The faster he moved, the less likely it was that he would encounter others.

After a little while the mists began to thin, and looming up out of them was a great ring of standing stones. He knew them, for once, in the real world, Aranloth had invoked their magic and escaped from Lindercroft.

"How is it the standing stones are here, but not the ruins of the city?"

"There is an ebb and flow of chance to these things," his grandfather replied. "But also, the stones are linked to a very great magic. The reflection of things from the real world is better when magic is involved."

Faran glanced briefly at the stones. They brought back memories, but he had a task to fulfill and he went to move on.

"Wait a moment," his grandfather said.

"Aranloth is close," Faran replied. "I can feel it. The sooner I find him the better. Time is running out."

His grandfather removed his helm again, and his face was earnest.

"Even so, that must wait. There are things I must tell you."

Faran felt torn, but he agreed and they sat down, their backs to one of the stones and looking out to the ocean of fog that was slowly diminishing as some unseen movement of air dissipated it.

"Time is running out," his grandfather stated, "even as you say. But not just for Aranloth."

"What else is happening?"

"Many forces are at work over all the land. Some for the good, and others not. But this is what chiefly concerns you now. Druilgar has learned that Ferla is the seventh knight, and he believes it, as he should. But he does not know who you are, and it troubles him. However, the Dark will soon discover your secret."

"I have no secrets," Faran said. "There's nothing to discover."

"Are you so sure?"

Faran was at a loss. He knew he had no secrets, but his grandfather seemed so serious.

"Who are you?" his grandfather spoke into the silence.

"I don't understand. You know who I am."

His grandfather looked out toward where the great falls sped off the escarpment, if the thinning fog had not obscured them.

"You are a young man, and a warrior. Also a magician, and maybe a lòhren one day. You are a Kingshield Knight also, if you choose to be. Or not. But either way you are a knight, for you fight against evil. And you are something more, too."

Faran felt a cold fear creep upon him. "What else am I?"

His grandfather did not answer directly. "Ferla said that she would kill the knights, but she did not say she would kill the king. Foresight touched her then. But why would she not try to kill the king? He is a Kingshield Knight also."

Faran shook his head mutely. He had not considered this before.

"She knew, in her heart, that the battle with the king would fall to you."

"But why? I'm not the seventh knight?"

"Because it would be fitting. Ferla does not know this, and she was merely the voice of destiny when she claimed her right as the seventh knight. But the king is left to you, for you are descended in direct line from the brother of the first king of Faladir. The present king has killed all his relatives. At least the ones he knows. You are the last man of his blood left, and when he discovers that…"

Faran could not believe it. "I'm not descended of royalty. I'm descended from you."

"And I am descended from the first king's brother. Conlar his name was. His wife was Cerwen. They dwelt in ages past in Dromdruin as did we, and over the years their line mixed with that of the villagers and knowledge of it was lost. At least, to most. But Aranloth knew, and he advised my family to keep our heritage secret. He knew that this day would come."

Faran did not know what to say.

"It's a lot to take in, my boy," his grandfather said. "But you can believe it, and that is why you must kill the king. You must do it first, for once he learns this secret he will move the world to kill you."

"But—"

"That is enough for now. Already I have delayed too long. You must find Aranloth, and quickly."

They stood up, and it seemed a little lighter than it had been. The fog was parting.

"One more thing," his grandfather said. "You are of royalty, and you should look like it. Whether you go to death or to victory, remember who you are and know that your ancestors were heroes." Even as his grandfather spoke, he raised his hand in a strange gesture and uttered a word of power.

Faran felt nothing, but when he looked down he saw that his cloak had become a deep crimson, the color of royalty. He was not surprised. Anything was possible in the void, and it was the least strange thing that had happened to him since crossing the dark-watered river.

They went on, and began to walk downhill. Faran could scarcely think, for the revelation of his heritage astounded him. But that soon changed.

He slowed. Aranloth was very close, but the void was changing every step they took. It was no longer desolate, but grass grew underfoot, green and springy. Sheep bleated in the distance, cows grazed peacefully and woods sprang up here and there over the slope. The mist rolled back, and sunlight shone down on a world of peace and wonder.

"This is surely no longer the void," Faran whispered.

His grandfather looked about as well, but did not seem surprised.

"It is the void. But what is different here is the presence of Aranloth. Now you begin to see how powerful he is. Even the void cannot subdue him nor overshadow his will with its own."

They kept walking downhill, and afar there was a glint of water as the great falls over the escarpment came into view, and the green angle that lay between the two rivers. This was a haven of peace, and Faran began to wonder what could induce Aranloth to leave it and return to the bitterness of the real world.

25. The Long Defeat

They found Aranloth by the side of a small wood, the great view to the escarpment and falls before him, and a small herd of sheep grazing contentedly around him. He leaned on his staff, as he often did, but now he looked like a shepherd with his crook rather than a lòhren with the scepter of his high order.

Aranloth nodded to them both as they approached, but his grandfather held back.

"This is your quest, Faran. I can play no part in it. But I will see you before you go."

Faran walked on alone. The sheep mostly ignored him, merely looking at him between bites of grass and the various broadleaved herbs in the pasture that they preferred.

"You should not have come here, Faran," the lòhren said. "The risks of the void are many, and it is no place for the living."

Faran drew to a stop before him. "You seem to have little fear of the risks of this place."

The old man shrugged. "The denizens of the void have learned to avoid me. But they will not pay you the same respect, I fear."

"So far, so good," Faran replied. "But it is not without good purpose that I have risked coming here."

"I know you think that, and I value that you have done so. But your risk is in vain, for I'll not go back."

"Will you stay here forever, then?"

"No one remains in the void for long. It is merely a place … between places."

Faran's worst fears were coming to fruition. This was not going to be like it was when he brought Ferla back from the void. She had *wanted* to leave it with him. But Aranloth had no intention of leaving at all.

"We should have gone back for you at the cabin by the lake," Faran said, "but we didn't know you were still alive."

Aranloth grimaced slightly as though at remembered pain.

"Not at all. You would have been killed. Kareste did exactly as she should have, and things have turned out well, even if not quite as you expected. Ferla has claimed the title of seventh knight, and you have learned skills to strike fear into your enemies. And they do, you know. Fear you, that is."

"Perhaps they do, but that doesn't stop them from hunting us. They'll never give up, as you warned long ago. We need you. Both Ferla and myself. We need you, and Alithoras needs you."

Aranloth sighed. "You don't need me. Alithoras doesn't need me. Others can take my place. You yourself have become formidable, as has Ferla. I'll not say that your fight against the Shadow is easy. It's not. But you have a chance of victory, and that's as much as I could give you."

The sheep moved away a little, grazing farther down the slope, and Aranloth watched them serenely. He was the lòhren Faran had always known, but different at the same time.

"You underestimate yourself, Aranloth."

"I do not think so."

"You do. If you were there to guide us, our chances of success would be higher. No one knows all that you know, or can do all that you can do. We really do need you."

The old man lost some of that appearance of serenity, and a haunted look crossed his face and then was gone.

171

"The world has always needed me," he replied. "And I have endured sorrow and pain and torment for years beyond count. Do you know what it is like to watch a friend age and die? Do you know how it feels to see a nation rise and prosper only to succumb to corruption? Can you envision what it is like to fight against the evils of the world, and suffer the long defeat? For the evils I fought in my youth still exist now."

The old man looked away, and there was a glimmer of tears in his eyes. Faran felt some of the emotion that must be roiling through the lòhren, but he knew it was only the tiniest sliver of the enormity of what the old man felt.

"I'm sorry," he said. "You're right, and I should not have come. I had no right to ask you to come back. None at all. You have already given us everything."

Aranloth did not speak for a time. Then he pointed his staff out toward the escarpment.

"Do you see that land down there? It is my home. Or it was before all Alithoras became my concern. Is it not beautiful?"

Faran gazed out, taking in the green angle between the two rivers, the great falls and the mighty escarpment.

"It is. I like it, but I like Dromdruin more."

Aranloth smiled. "Indeed. That was your home, and where you grew up. It will always be in your blood. But for you and I there is no going back. Home is lost to us."

Faran answered slowly. "But you are here, now. In your home."

"In a manner of speaking. It's not real though. Nothing in the void is. All is illusion."

"So it is in the real world also," Faran answered. "Few things are as they seem, and reality is but perception."

The old man laughed. "I taught you well! What you say is true."

172

Faran did not want to leave, but he knew he must. If he spent too long in the void, he would never be able to return. Already, Aranloth could not return without someone to bring him back, and soon Faran would be in the same position.

"Again, I'm sorry, Aranloth. We were selfish. We wanted you back to help us. But we also wanted you back because we missed you. We had no right to ask, though."

They shook hands in the warrior's grip, and then Faran walked away. In the distance, he saw his grandfather waiting. He was another one he would never see again, and for a moment Faran felt what it would be like to be Aranloth. To live through all those long years and to lose so many he loved. Small wonder that he embraced death rather than the pain of living.

Aranloth called out to him before he had left the little fold of pasture.

"Did you really miss me?"

Faran turned back. The old man no longer leaned on his staff, and the green grass and sheep were gone. The desolation of the void was about him.

"I missed you. And I know Ferla and Kareste did as well. We always will."

The lòhren straightened as though he had reached a decision.

"Perhaps I have been the selfish one. And maybe I am not done with the long fight yet. There have been many victories to offset the advancing Shadow, and maybe I have a part to play in one more."

Faran felt stunned. He had thought his quest failed, but something had reached the heart of the old man, and he was glad of it.

"Come back with me Aranloth, and we'll set a blaze under the backsides of the enemy and make them hop!"

173

The old man laughed. "You've been spending too much time with Kubodin!"

They went to join Faran's grandfather, and then they hastened back up to the top of the slope.

"Your time grows short," his grandfather said. "We must hasten."

Faran knew that was true. Already he felt different. The void was becoming more real to him than it had been, and the real world more dreamlike.

They traveled swiftly. The mists swirled around them again, and the dust of their passage over the desolate land hung lifelessly in the air behind them.

"There are eyes upon us," Aranloth said.

Faran saw nothing, and even his grandfather looked around, seemingly unsure where the enemy was.

Aranloth pointed ahead down the track where the fog was thick.

"There," he said. A light blazed from the tip of his staff, and the fog rolled away. Revealed was a group of figures, tall and gaunt. Black cloaks they wore, and in their hands were dark staffs, twisted and curled grotesquely. But what drew Faran's gaze was their faces. These were bloated and rotting, like a carcass left in the sun for several days.

"Elùgroths," he whispered, but it was a question rather than a statement.

"So they are," Aranloth answered, "and in the void the evil that is in them shows itself."

Their leader shuffled forward, and he spoke in a commanding voice.

"You will not pass."

Aranloth looked at them, and there was anger in his gaze. Gone was the look of the serene shepherd that he had worn before. This was Aranloth the lòhren, master of ancient lore and bane of the Dark since the days of the Letharn empire.

"I *will* pass," he answered softly, but there was steel in his voice and a faint glow emanated from him. To Faran, he was a figure of awesome power, but the elùgroths were many, and he drew his sword. There would be a fight here.

Aranloth walked forward. One of the dark figures raised his staff and crimson fire spurted from its tip. Yet Aranloth merely flicked his own and that red flame turned back like a crashing wave and consumed the elùgroth. The sorcerer screamed and writhed, the rotted flesh melted from him, and his bones blackened and scorched.

Aranloth kept walking, seemingly oblivious to the other elùgroths, and they receded into the fog and were gone.

Faran exchanged a look with his grandfather, and they sheathed their swords. It was a side to Aranloth that Faran at least had not seen before. Normally he was wary of fights, and tried hard to avoid them, but his power in the void seemed to be greater than it had been in Alithoras.

"Come along," the old man said, half turning. "They'll not dare trouble us again, and you must lead the way back, for I do not know it."

Faran took the lead then, and he retraced his steps. There were times when he himself was not sure of the way. The void seemed to have changed since he had entered it, and that sent a chill of fear through him.

Yet at length he found the dark river, and the little boat that he had hidden on the shore. This they pulled out and took to the edge of the dark water.

Faran turned to his grandfather. "Will I see you again?"

"The world is full of chances," came the reply. "Many ill, but some good. We will see. But remember your heritage, always. It marks you for death, but you are the

175

counterpoint to the king. Where he has fallen, you can restore honor and pride in our line."

Faran hugged him then, and Aranloth stepped forward and shook the knight's hand.

"The wrongs that were done to you may yet be avenged, and the people freed from tyranny."

"May it be so," the knight said, and he stepped back and the mists enveloped him.

They pushed the boat into the river then, and for all the ease with which Faran had crossed over earlier, it now seemed an impossible task to row back. The boat rode low in the water, as though a great weight burdened it, and the currents contrived to push it back to the shore. But once Faran reached the middle things grew easier, and though he felt exhaustion heavy upon him, he came to the far shore at length.

There they disembarked, and behind them the mists swirled dark and angry, but they turned away from that and back toward light and life.

26. Marked in the Void

Faran woke, and he remembered that he hung in the abyss suspended only by magic. Panic surged through him.

A hand gripped his shoulder. "Peace," Aranloth said. "You are safe."

Above him, he saw that Kareste was there, and her staff was in her hand. This she raised, and the myriad lights that suspended him and Aranloth swirled and shifted. They rose, lifting them both up gently until they could step onto the ledge of stone.

The lights flashed and swam in the abyss, a dazzling display brighter than the starry sky, and they twirled and spun out of sight into the darkness below.

"What *are* they?" Faran asked, in awe of the magic.

"The spirits of the Letharn dead, all of them who ever lived, bound to the tombs in life eternal."

This was more than Faran expected, and his mind grasped at the complexities and implications of such magic, but fell short. It was beyond his fathoming.

Silently, Kareste hugged the old man. And he returned the embrace.

"Was I right to do this thing?" she asked.

Faran knew what she meant, and the old man pulled back a little and smiled at her.

"You were right. Do not doubt it, ever. I have lived years beyond count, but I still have more to do." He looked at Faran and an understanding passed between them. Kareste need not know that he was at first reluctant to return.

She turned her gaze to Faran, and then to his surprise hugged him as well.

"You did well, Faran. Twice you have been to the void and returned. That takes courage and skill. Alithoras owes you for what you have done, and I owe you." She stepped back and looked him up and down. "And what is this?"

At first, he did not know what she meant, but then he saw that his cloak remained the crimson that his grandfather had turned it in the void.

"His grandfather told him who he is," Aranloth said. "At least I believe so. Is that not right, Faran?"

"He did. Did you both know?"

"Of course. It was a secret long held in your family. Only I knew, and in turn I told Kareste. That secret kept you safe. Or at least safer."

It seemed that everyone had been keeping secrets from Faran, but he was old enough and wise enough now to understand why. He did not hold it against them, and what did it matter anyway? He still had a task to do, and that had not changed.

Kareste turned to Aranloth. "Are you well enough to travel?" she asked.

"You have slept the death-sleep. You tell me."

She grinned at him. "I think you're ready, and the enemy will rue having pushed you into the sleep. Let them beware!"

Faran glanced at Aranloth. He looked as he always did, a hale old man who was stronger even than he seemed. Yet there was more about him now. Some indefinable sense of power and confidence that had always been hidden but was now closer to the surface. But it was hard to be sure.

The lòhren's robes were also surprising. They should have been dirty from travel and tattered from battle. Yet they gleamed whiter than he had ever seen before.

"Had I known you lived," Kareste said suddenly, "I would have come to aid you."

"Then it is best that you did not know," Aranloth answered. "Your duty was to Faran and Ferla rather than me. And you have done well with them. So too Asana and Kubodin."

Faran was confused by this. That Aranloth knew of their training, he had revealed in the void, but there had been no time there to ask questions. "How do you know that we trained with Asana and Kubodin?"

"That was the plan that I had formulated for you, yet the death-sleep has its advantages as well as dangers. I saw much, and learned many things."

Aranloth would not be drawn to say more on that, and they had no wish to linger in the tombs. So it was that they began to walk out, but not the way they had come in.

Kareste led, and she took them farther along the path that they had started, only now the narrow shelf rose up out of the abyss and came to a long tunnel.

This they followed. It climbed steeply, but it swerved at times for no reason that Faran could see, yet he supposed that the ancient Letharn did nothing without purpose and there would be a reason here whether he understood it or not.

At first, Aranloth walked slowly, and they halted regularly for short rests. But as they went on the old man seemed to gain greater strength, and his eyes gleamed in the dark.

After some time, the tunnel leveled out. It branched out into crossroads and forks, and here Aranloth took the lead and walked with confidence.

"We'll leave by a northern exit," he said as he walked. "It's safer than the way you were forced to come in."

Faran had guessed that already, but he was glad of it too. He had no wish to go back anywhere near the way he had come in.

The tunnels they followed soon changed, and they now had alcoves cut into the walls. They were in the tombs proper now, and the dead were interred here.

"Touch nothing," Aranloth warned. Faran had not forgotten the poison that coated the treasures lying with the dead, but it was a warning better heard often than not at all.

He did not wish to look into the alcoves, but from time to time he could not help himself. When he did glance that way, he was surprised. This area of the tombs seemed to be the resting place of warriors. Their preserved bodies, nearly lifelike, lay on raised slabs of stone. Spears stood propped up beside them, seemingly ready to hand for use. Swords were sheathed at their sides, and armor protected their bodies. Helms were on their heads, and even at times he fancied he saw the whites of their eyes as they watched him march by.

He vowed not to look again. But the dead drew his gaze, and he could not help himself.

"Have no fear," Aranloth murmured. "You wear armor like theirs, and they would treat you as a brother."

If Aranloth had intended that to ease his anxiety, he was mistaken. It only raised it. But at length they passed into a different section and here craftsmen lay direct on the stone floor. They had no weapons about them, but only the tools of their trade. Nor did they give Faran the impression that they might rise from their thousands of years of sleep to ask who these intruders were who disturbed them.

They branched to the left, and a sudden scent of fresh air caressed Faran's face. They must be close to the exit now, and he willed it to be so. He felt deathly tired, and

180

he wondered how long he and Kareste had been down here without sleep. A day? More? But escape was close now, and then they could cast themselves down and rest.

His spirit was at a low ebb, and lethargy dulled his eyes. His legs shuffled forward, and his head was bowed with fatigue. Even at that moment the harakgar chose to attack.

The Three Sisters came flying down the tunnel before them. Fire flared around them, and their eyes blazed with righteous fury. Their curved daggers gleamed in their hands, sharp and wicked, but their rictus mouths showed long teeth, sharper still.

Faran stood still, caught by surprise. But Aranloth flung up a hand and his voice boomed out loud enough to deafen and cause stone dust to shake loose from the ceiling.

"*Har nere ferork. Skigg gar see!*"

It was the charm that controlled the harakgar, but never had Faran seen it have such effect before. The three of them shrieked, and they placed their hands to their ears and fled into the dark.

Aranloth lowered his hand. "They'll not trouble us again," he said with confidence.

Faran had not thought to ever see the harakgar banished so swiftly.

"You are changed," he said to the old man. "You are stronger than you were."

Aranloth looked thoughtful. "I'm not altered. But you first met me when I was weak. This is the true version of myself, but weak or strong I am the same."

There was truth in that. Aranloth's character had not changed. But there was a sense of power about him now always, whereas before it was only there in glimpses. This version of him could never pass as Nuatha the healer, as he had once done.

They moved ahead then, and Aranloth led the way with certain steps. He knew where he was going, and Faran did not doubt that he could navigate these tombs blindfolded.

The air became fresher still, and momentarily there was light ahead. Aranloth walked steadily toward it, seemingly unconcerned, but Faran and Ferla both looked around with great caution. This was the last chance for the harakgar to attack again, but there was no sign of them.

They came out into the light. It was late in the afternoon, and the sun was lowering to their left. Opposite them yawned the great chasm and on the far side the cliffs with their massive carvings of grandeur. Faran felt again the awe he had the first time he saw them. It was not something anyone could get used to seeing, but stronger even than that was the sense of freedom. He had escaped the tombs, and he breathed in deep of the air like a man released from a dungeon after years of servitude.

The ledge was not large, but it seemed huge to him. It spoke to a sense of freedom, and the stele with the strange writing on it did not disturb him as it had last time.

Nearly, he sank to the ground to rest, but Aranloth stiffened beside him.

"Beware!"

Faran looked around, but he observed nothing out of place. Then he saw, coming down the narrow trail to the left, Sofanil. With him was a band of elugs, and their faces were hideous with glee.

Quickly he glanced to the right, but coming up the trail was another band of elugs, a thick fog behind them rising up from the great falls and the water below.

Faran realized he was trapped, unless he and the others went back into the tombs. But Sofanil gestured, and a wall of flame shot up over the dark entrance. The knight had thought of that, and Faran felt his heart sink.

But he did take some heart. Looking at the elugs, and even the knight, they showed signs of fatigue. They had forced a march to get here in time, but how did they even know where to come? It was not possible.

Faran thought to buy some time. It would give him a chance to rest, and maybe Aranloth an opportunity to clear the flames preventing access to the tombs.

"How did you find me, Sofanil?"

The knight came to a stop, the elugs standing behind him on the narrow trail.

"I marked your spirit as you entered the void, and now there is no place on earth where I cannot find you. It is a powerful magic, but being in the void made it easy. A small mistake for you to make, maybe. But also your last. This is where it finally ends for you."

Faran remembered how the knight had ambushed him on first entering the void, and he cursed himself for a fool. He knew something had been done then, but he had forgotten to mention it to either Aranloth or Kareste. Now, they might die with him for his error.

Sofanil began to close in again, and his elugs came with him. They were tired, which was plain to see, but there was a certain eagerness in their steps too. They had been led on a long hunt, and now they planned on enjoying their revenge.

Below, the other group of elugs advanced also. The trap was closing, and there was no way out except by a fight, and it was not one likely to end in success. Not for three against so many.

Faran drew his sword, and the lethargy of the long journey in the tombs lifted off him. He would die fighting, and if he could, he would take Sofanil with him. That would be one less enemy for Ferla to face.

But before he could make any move Aranloth stepped forward. If the lòhren felt fear, he did not show it. Instead, he seemed at perfect ease. He raised his staff and pointed at Sofanil, but he did not attack. Rather, he spoke, and his voice rang out loud enough so that it echoed in the chasm below and lent an eeriness to his warning. For it was a warning he gave instead of a plea for mercy.

27. Reunited

"Beware!" Aranloth cried. "Your doom is nearly upon you, Sofanil. Retreat, and you yet may live. Come forward, and you will die."

Sofanil laughed. "I am not who I once was, Aranloth, to be awed by your words. On a time, I would have believed you. Now I know better and follow a different master."

"I never lied to you, Sofanil. And I do not now. This is no trick, and I give you fair warning. Go back, and live. You have become an enemy, but while you still breathe there is hope you may repent."

The knight seemed to consider that. "Tell me truthfully, for once we were close. Have you seen a vision? Do you share a foretelling?"

Aranloth did not falter. "I have seen no vision, nor do I foretell. But assuredly, I know your death approaches swift as an arrow, unless you flee it."

Sofanil hesitated, then he shook his head. "You sadden me, old man. Once I would have believed anything you said, but now I have learned better. You would lie to me, and that I cannot tolerate. You will die, and your companions also. You would have anyway, but it would have been more noble of you to fight rather than to try to deceive."

Aranloth stepped farther out onto the stone shelf until he stood before the knight that had once been his pupil. All gazes followed him, waiting to see what he would do.

"This is your final warning, Sofanil. Take it, I beg of you."

The knight looked at him, but he showed no sign of changing his mind.

"Do you intend to duel with me, old man? You are a fool as well as a liar. You are spent, and I am rising on a wave of sorcery such as you could not imagine."

Aranloth sighed. "How little you know, and how badly you learned your lessons from me." Then the lòhren slowly went down on one knee.

Sofanil seemed surprised. "Now you would—"

But he got no further. Flashing in the lowering rays of the sun sped a gleaming arrow shaft. Steel headed it, and the fletching at its tail thrummed. It passed above Aranloth's lowered form, flashing through the space where he had stood only moments ago, and then came the thud as it hit its target.

Sofanil staggered back, the arrow having torn out his throat, smashed into the vertebra and continued on. Blood gushed and foamed. It was a mortal wound, and one that should have seen him fall instantly. But instead, he staggered forward.

Crimson fire dripped from the knight's fingers, and he gestured strangely, sending the fire scattering outward. All about him confusion broke out, but the elugs did not flee.

Aranloth raised his staff, and a shield of silver-white plumed before him protectively. Even so, he was knocked back by the force of the attack.

Faran glanced back whence the arrow had sped. Down the narrow trail he looked, past the elugs and into the mist boiling up from the waters far below. Ferla stepped out of it, and his heart soared. Then came Asana and Kubodin. Their swords flashed, and elugs died.

The din of battle broke out, and chaos descended in a storm of fury. Kareste sent a stream of lòhren-fire hurtling at the dying knight, but he smashed it aside and sent his own riposte which Kareste ducked.

186

The wicked stream of crimson fire shot over her head and struck the wall of flame at the entrance to the tombs. Those magics boomed like thunder as they met and flew unraveling into the tunnels.

Faran was half deafened by the noise, but he was moving. His sword flickered and a charging elug died in a spray of blood.

The press of battle was joined. Swords screamed against swords, magic repelled sorcery and the dead fell to the earth or staggered unwittingly into the chasm to plunge onto the jagged rocks far below.

Those elugs lower down the trail were pressed up, and Faran glimpsed Asana and Kubodin. One hacked with his axe and the other moved like a dancer, swaying and slashing. But dead elugs fell before them like scythed grass in a meadow. Behind them on the narrow trail Ferla stood calmly, winging arrows of death into the heart of the maelstrom.

An elug hammered at Faran with a mighty blow, but he nimbly sidestepped and his own sword cut, severing an arm. The stump pulsed blood, but then the creature fell as the artery in his thigh was severed less than a heartbeat later.

Faran swung around, looking for more foes. The last of them reeled away though, burning like a torch from a strike of lòhren-fire.

Only Sofanil still stood of that group on the higher part of the trail. How he yet lived, Faran was not sure. But the knight sent another spray of fire at Kareste, and again she dodged out of the way. Once more the sorcery hurtled into the mouth of the tombs, and a deep rumble came from within them like the exhalation of a breath, and dust spewed out of the entrance.

Faran sprang toward Sofanil, but even as he did so Ferla must have seen a clear view of the knight. Another arrow sped across the gap. This one took him through the eye slit in his helm, then another sprouted from his inner thigh and his lifeblood wetted the stone trail.

The knight went down, trying to scream, but only bloody foam escaped his mouth, flecking his mail shirt. Then he tried to rise again, but only came halfway up before he toppled once more and lay still.

A deep silence descended. The battle was ended, and Faran knew that somehow he had cheated death. As had his companions.

Aranloth stood, leaning on his staff, and he gazed sadly at his dead pupil. For all that they were enemies now, Faran knew that once the old man had taught him just as he more recently had taught himself and Ferla.

Kareste stood watching the old man, her own expression sad, but more likely for the pain she knew Aranloth suffered than at the death of Sofanil.

But then, looking down the trail, Faran saw Asana and Kubodin walk up it toward him. His heart soared to see them, but he only had eyes for Ferla coming up behind them.

He walked down to meet them halfway, and he took off his helm. Ferla did likewise, and the sight of her red hair spilling out and her own gaze meeting his sent a shiver through his body. He embraced her, holding her tight, and then he kissed her. This seemed to surprise her as much as it did him, but she kissed him back.

They did not speak when finally they pulled away, but merely studied each other. Asana and Kubodin were silent too, but the little warrior from the hills fingered one of his earrings and winked at Faran.

More dust billowed out from the entrance to the tombs, and then a slow rumble sounded from deep in the earth.

"Magic has stirred dangerous forces within the tombs," Aranloth called out. Even as he spoke the earth trembled. On the far side of the chasm, one of the great carvings shivered and rocks fell, tumbling and crashing into the ravine far below.

"Fly!" Aranloth cried. "This whole ledge might collapse!"

They ran. Faran was exhausted, but fear lent him strength. Downward he raced, and the others were with him. The mist out of which Ferla had emerged was now faded away. It had only ever been a small patch, enough to hide his three friends and he realized it had been summoned for that purpose alone. But it was gone, and they could see better without it.

Yet night was falling, and a misstep here could mean death. It was a long way down though, and the narrow way thrummed beneath his feet and dust and rocks began to fall from above.

Thus ends *The Scarlet Knight*. The Kingshield series continues in book six, *The Sacred Knight*. Therein, Faran and Ferla will face ultimate evil, and the final battle for the future of Faladir will be fought…

THE SACRED KNIGHT

BOOK SIX OF THE KINGSHIELD SERIES

COMING SOON

Amazon lists millions of titles, and I'm glad you discovered this one. But if you'd like to know when I release a new book, instead of leaving it to chance, sign up for my new release list. I'll send you an email on publication.

Yes please! – Go to www.homeofhighfantasy.com and sign up.

No thanks – I'll take my chances.

Dedication

There's a growing movement in fantasy literature. Its name is noblebright, and it's the opposite of grimdark.

Noblebright celebrates the virtues of heroism. It's an old-fashioned thing, as old as the first story ever told around a smoky campfire beneath ancient stars. It's storytelling that highlights courage and loyalty and hope for the spirit of humanity. It recognizes the dark, the dark in us all, and the dark in the villains of its stories. It recognizes death, and treachery and betrayal. But it dwells on none of these things.

I dedicate this book, such as it is, to that which is noblebright. And I thank the authors before me who held the torch high so that I could see the path: J.R.R. Tolkien, C.S. Lewis, Terry Brooks, David Eddings, Susan Cooper, Roger Taylor and many others. I salute you.

And, for a time, I too shall hold the torch high.

Appendix: Encyclopedic Glossary

Note: the glossary of each book in this series is individualized for that book alone. Additionally, there is often historical material provided in its entries for people, artifacts and events that are not included in the main text.

Many races dwell in Alithoras. All have their own language, and though sometimes related to one another the changes sparked by migration, isolation and various influences often render these tongues unintelligible to each other.

The ascendancy of Halathrin culture, combined with their widespread efforts to secure and maintain allies against elug incursions, has made their language the primary means of communication between diverse peoples.

This glossary contains a range of names and terms. Many are of Halathrin origin, and their meaning is provided. The remainder derive from native tongues and are obscure, so meanings are only given intermittently.

Often, names of Camar and Halathrin elements are combined. This is especially so for the aristocracy. Few other tribes had such long-term friendship with the immortal Halathrin as the Camar, and though in this relationship they lost some of their natural culture, they gained nobility and knowledge in return.

List of abbreviations:

Cam. Camar

Comb. Combined

Cor. Corrupted form

Chg: Cheng

Hal. Halathrin

Leth. Letharn

Prn. Pronounced

Alithoras: *Hal.* "Silver land." The Halathrin name for the continent they settled after leaving their own homeland. Refers to the extensive river and lake systems they found and their wonder at the beauty of the land.

Aranloth: *Hal.* "Noble might." A lòhren of ancient heritage. Travels Alithoras under different names and guises.

Asana: *Chg.* "Gift of light." Rumored to be the greatest sword master in the history of the Cheng people. His father was a Duthenor tribesman.

Barlan: *Cam.* "Bee wolf – a poetic expression for a bear." A Kingshield Knight.

Bouncing Stone (the): An ancient inn built at the same time as the Tower of the Stone. It is said a smithy occupied the land previously, and here of old attempts were made to destroy the Morleth Stone.

Caludreth: *Cam.* "Lord of the waves." A poetic term in Camar literature for a ship. Once a Kingshield Knight.

Carist Nien: *Hal.* "Ice river." A river of northern Alithoras that has its source in the hills of Lòrenta.

Cerwen: *Cam.* "Peace of the forest glade." An unusual name in Faladir where most are related to oceanic terms. A hunter of skill and renown who married Prince Conlar. Legend claims that she came as a stranger to Faladir from a distant land.

Conduil: *Cam.* Etymology obscure. The first king of Faladir. He broke the Siege of Faladir and founded the order of Kingshield Knights, of which he was the first.

Conlar: *Cam.* Etymology obscure. The younger brother of the first king of Faladir. Renowned as a mighty warrior. Husband to Cerwen. Rumored in his later years to have acquired skill in magic.

Death-sleep: A state of suspended animation used by lòhrens of the highest order to heal from terrible wounds. It also prolongs life, for it allows the body to repair itself. It requires great skill and magic, but the practice is not without extreme risks. Especially to the mind.

Dromdruin: *Cam.* "Valley of the ancient woods." One of many valleys in the realm of Faladir. Home of Faran, and birthplace throughout the history of the realm of many Kingshield Knights.

Druilgar: *Hal.* "Spear star – a comet." King of Faladir, and First Knight of the Kingshield Knights. Descendent of King Conduil.

Elves: See Halathrin.

Elù-drak: *Hal.* "Shadow wings." A creature of the Dark. Deadly, and used by sorcerers to gather information and assassinate chosen victims. The female of the species is the most dangerous, having the power to inspire terror and bend victims to her will. Few can resist. Of old, even great warriors succumbed and willingly let the creature take their life. One of the more terrible creatures of the Old World.

Elùdrath: *Hal.* "Shadowed Lord." A sorcerer. First and greatest among elùgroths. Believed to be dead or defeated. Yet the order of lòhrens guards against his return.

Elùgai: *Hal. Prn.* Eloo-guy. "Shadowed force." The sorcery of an elùgroth.

Elù-haraken: *Hal.* "Shadowed wars." Long ago battles in a time that is become myth to the scattered Camar tribes.

Faladir: *Cam.* "Fortress of Light." A Camar city founded out of the ruinous days of the elù-haraken.

Faran: *Cam.* "Spear of the night – a star." A name of good luck. Related to the name Dardenath, though of a later layer of linguistic change. A young hunter from Dromdruin valley. His grandfather was a Kingshield Knight, though not the first of their ancestors to be so.

Ferla: *Cam.* "Unforeseen bounty." A young hunter from Dromdruin Valley.

195

First Knight: The designated leader of the Kingshield Knights.

Grundar: *Cam.* "Saw-toothed fish – a member of the sturgeon family." Once a farmer but now a prospering merchant.

Halathrin: *Hal.* "People of Halath." A race of elves named after an honored lord who led an exodus of his people to the land of Alithoras in pursuit of justice, having sworn to defeat a great evil. They are human, though of fairer form, greater skill and higher culture. They possess a unity of body, mind and spirit that enables insight and endurance beyond the native races of Alithoras. Said to be immortal, but killed in great numbers during their conflicts in ancient times with the evil they sought to destroy. Those conflicts are collectively known as the Shadowed Wars.

Harakgar (the): *Leth.* "The Three Sisters." Creatures of magic brought into being by the Letharn. Their purpose is to protect the tombs of their creators from robbery.

Hundred (the): A resistance group established in Faladir to prepare the way for the coming of the seventh knight.

Kareste: *Hal.* "Ice unlocking – the spring thaw." A lòhren of mysterious origin. Friend to Aranloth, but usually more active farther north in Alithoras than Faladir.

Kingshield Knights: An order of knights founded by King Conduil. Their sacred task is to guard the indestructible Morleth Stone from theft and use by the evil forces of the world. They are more than great warriors, being trained in philosophy and the arts also. In addition to their prime function as guards, they travel the land at whiles dispensing justice and offering of their wisdom and council.

Kubodin: *Chg.* Etymology unknown. A wild hillman from the lands of the Cheng. Simple appearing, but far more than he seems. Asana's manservant.

Letharn: *Hal.* "Stone raisers. Builders." A race of people that in antiquity conquered most of Alithoras. Now, only faint traces of their civilization endure.

Lindercroft: *Cam.* "Rising mountain crashes – a wave rolling into the seashore." A Kingshield Knight. Youngest of the order.

Lòhren: *Hal. Prn.* Ler-ren. "Knowledge giver – a counselor." Other terms used by various nations include wizard, druid and sage.

Lòhren-fire: A defensive manifestation of lòhrengai. The color of the flame varies according to the skill and temperament of the lòhren.

Lòhrenin: *Hal.* "Council of lòhrens."

Lòrenta: *Hal.* "Hills of knowledge." Uplands in northern Alithoras where the lòhrens maintain a fortress.

Magic: Mystic power. See lòhrengai and elùgai.

Menendil: *Hal.* "Sign of hope." Sometimes called Mender. His is an old family, and he can trace his lineage back to the days before the founding of Faladir to a liegeman of the then chieftain. Unusually, his name is not of Camar origin. Family history records that his forefather was a seer, and was greatly esteemed by his lord.

Morleth Stone: *Hal.* "Round stone." The name signifies that such a stone is not natural. It is formed by elùgai for sorcerous purposes. The stone is strengthened by arcane power to act as a receptacle of enormous force. Little is known of their making and uses except that they are rare and that elùgroths perish during their construction. The stone guarded by the Kingshield Knights in Faladir is said to be the most powerful of all that were created. And to be sentient.

Norgril: *Cam.* "Leaping fish." A member of the Hundred.

Norla: *Cam.* "Fish hunter – fisherman." Wife of Menendil.

Nuatha: *Cam.* "Silver wanderer – a stream." A vagabond healer who travels widely throughout Faladir. Aranloth in one of his guises.

Nurthil Wood: *Cam.* "Dark secrets." A great forest north of Faladir. Home to outlaws and disaffected from the wide lands all around. Once, a stronghold of the forces of darkness, but cleansed by succeeding kings of Faladir.

Osahka: *Leth.* "The guide – specifically a spiritual or moral guide." A title of enormous reverence and respect. Applied to Aranloth for his role as spiritual leader of the Kingshield Knights.

Savanest: *Cam.* "Subtle skill." A Kingshield Knight. All the knights think of each other as brothers. But Savanest and Sofanil are also brothers by blood.

Shadow Fliers: See elù-drak.

Shadowed Lord (the): Once, a lòhren. But he succumbed to evil and pursued forbidden knowledge and powers. He created an empire of darkness and struck to conquer all Alithoras during the elù-haraken. He was defeated, but his magic had become greater than any ever known. Some say he will return from death to finish the war he started. Whether that is so, no one knows. But the order of lòhrens guard against it, and many evils that served him yet live.

Shadowed Wars: See elù-haraken.

Sofanil: *Cam.* "Sharp of wits." A Kingshield Knight. All the knights think of each other as brothers. But Sofanil and Savanest are also brothers by blood.

Sorcerer: See elùgroth.

Sorcery: See elùgai.

Stonard: *Cam.* "A beach of gravel rather than sand." Captain of a mercenary band in service to Knight Barlan.

Three Sisters: See harakgar.

Tower of the Stone: The tower King Conduil caused to be built to serve as the guarding structure of the Morleth Stone. Some claim his sarcophagus rests upon its pinnacle, as it was the custom of some ancient Camar royalty to be interred on a high place where the lights of the sun, moon and stars still lit their long sleep.

Were-beast: A creature of the shadow. Said to be able to shapeshift from animal to human form.

Were-hound: A creature of the shadow that takes the form of a dog.

Wizard: See lòhren.

About the author

I'm a man born in the wrong era. My heart yearns for faraway places and even further afield times. Tolkien had me at the beginning of *The Hobbit* when he said, ". . . one morning long ago in the quiet of the world . . ."

Sometimes I imagine myself in a Viking mead-hall. The long winter night presses in, but the shimmering embers of a log in the hearth hold back both cold and dark. The chieftain calls for a story, and I take a sip from my drinking horn and stand up . . .

Or maybe the desert stars shine bright and clear, obscured occasionally by wisps of smoke from burning camel dung. A dry gust of wind marches sand grains across our lonely campsite, and the wayfarers about me stir restlessly. I sip cool water and begin to speak.

I'm a storyteller. A man to paint a picture by the slow music of words. I like to bring faraway places and times to life, to make hearts yearn for something they can never have, unless for a passing moment.

Printed in Great Britain
by Amazon